How she wanted h

"We're older now," No

"Wiser." One eyebrow rose. Dylan's hands settled on the outside of her knees and skimmed their way up her thighs, pausing on her hips.

"We won't make the same mistakes we made before."

"So you're saying..."

The force of her need for him shook the fingers she slid up his biceps. What would it feel like to have this officer obey her every wicked whim? If she was in charge, surely she wouldn't be as vulnerable... in danger...of giving him everything, including her heart.

"I can't fight this, Dylan." The fire he'd ignited inside her two weeks ago, the one that continued to smolder, could no longer be contained. The sensual flames licking over her flesh confirmed her assessment. "If we keep things physical only, we can indulge a little while you're here." Her eyes dipped to his hard, handsome mouth.

"We shouldn't waste the time we have left together."

Dear Reader,

The wintry Bering Sea has never seen such a heat wave as when Nolee Arnauyq reunites with her first love, USCG rescue swimmer POV 1 Dylan Holt... and ends up igniting a relationship that's too hot to handle!

Rookie crab-fishing boat captain Nolee has a lot to prove on her first season at the wheel. She doesn't want to be saved, thank you very much, yet professional rescuer Dylan has an aggravating habit of showing up just at the right—or wrong—moment. She can't turn down his offer to help when an accident leaves her short-handed on deck, yet how can she focus on scoring a big catch when she's wondering if it might be Dylan she wants to net most of all?

If you're a fan of the Discovery Channel's *Deadliest Catch* series like me, you're sure to love this high-stakes, steamy adrenaline rush of a romance aboard Nolee's vessel, the *Pacific Dawn*. Visit me at karenrock.com to learn more about my future releases or to let me know what you think of this book. I'd love to hear from you!

Happy reading!

Karen Rock

Karen Rock

His Last Defense

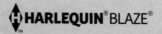

Recycling programs
for this product may
not exist in your area.

ISBN-13: 978-0-373-79961-9

His Last Defense

Printed in U.S.A.

www.Harlequin.com

Karen Rock is an award-winning young adult and adult contemporary author. She holds a master's degree in English and worked as an ELA instructor before becoming a full-time author. Most recently, her Harlequin Heartwarming novels have won the 2015 National Excellence in Romance Fiction Award and the 2015 Booksellers' Best Award. When she's not writing, Karen loves scouring estate sales, cooking and hiking. She lives in the Adirondack Mountain region with her husband, daughter and Cavalier King Charles spaniels. Visit her at karenrock.com.

Books by Karen Rock

Harlequin Heartwarming

Wish Me Tomorrow

His Hometown Girl

Someone Like You

A League of Her Own

Raising the Stakes

Winter Wedding Bells

"The Kiss"

His Kind of Cowgirl

Under an Adirondack Sky

Harlequin Blaze

His to Protect

To get the inside scoop on Harlequin Blaze and its talented writers, visit Facebook.com/BlazeAuthors.

All backlist available in ebook format.

Visit the Author Profile page at Harlequin.com for more titles.

To the USCG sea and air rescuers and the badass crab crews and captains who risk their lives every day on the treacherous Bering Sea. Your bold, adventurous lives are an inspiration. Special thanks to USCG commander Bill Friday, as well as the *Time Bandit*'s captain, Jonathan Hillstrand, and his fiancée, Sheryl, for their patient help in fact-checking. I never could have done it without you!

1

"WATCH OUT ON the bow!" Captain Nolee Arnauyq hollered into the mic of her crab-fishing boat, her heart beating every which way.

Below the wheelhouse, brightly clad deckhands scrambled for cover as gale-force winds whipped the Bering Sea, hurtling waves at the *Pacific Sun*. "Move it!" she yelled over the PA system.

The last man's yellow slicker disappeared under the overhang just as another wave smashed the rail. It pummeled the wooden deck and metal gear, sweeping high across Nolee's windows, obliterating her view of the black day.

Come on. Come on...

Her fingers tightened on the throttle as the vessel pitched in twenty-foot swells, buffeted by forty-five-knot winds. She peered through the streaming water. Despite the frigid late December temperature, the air inside the wheelhouse pressed, warm and humid. A trickle of sweat wound down her cheek. The weather maps hadn't predicted the massive winter storm would jog this far west.

Focus.

Grab crab. Get your men home safe.

If the tempest dragged the deckhands overboard, she wouldn't be able to locate them fast enough. Paralyzing hypothermia would take hold within minutes, death in five to ten.

"Everybody okay out there?" she called to the crew. One, two, three…four and five…six…she counted then recounted as they emerged, her nerves jangling.

"Rock and roll!" her barrel-chested deck boss, Everett, shouted, giving her a thumbs-up. After nine years of toiling alongside him, first as a deckhand and then as relief captain before her recent promotion, Nolee knew he never backed down from extreme weather challenges.

And neither did she.

Despite everything, she couldn't help but smile a bit at the amount of testosterone being thrown around—almost as much as the crab they'd caught. The undaunted gang took advantage of the momentary lull in the gale to bait another pot then drop it into the roiling sea. In a flash, the cage disappeared beneath the chop and its red marker and buoy grew indistinct as she steamed northwest on the edge of the unpredictable storm.

She slugged hot black coffee, burning her tongue, then jotted down the coordinates for this latest set on the string of pots and squinted into the gale. The tattered edges of her mast's American flag whipped in the air.

The hairs on her arms rose. Pricked. Sometimes, she swore she could smell the ocean coming at her, a briny, deep-water scent that floated into her nose, her lungs, her blood. Sure enough, another wave rose; a roaring filled her ears.

"Off the rails," she ordered. "That means you, blue," she added to a staring, slack-jawed Tyler. She recalled her own growing pains as a teenage deckhand, how the numbing work back then had helped her heal her broken heart.

Or form a scab over it, anyway. With relief, she watched Tyler stumble after the older men who'd been grinding all morning since dawn.

More water crested the port side, sweeping beneath the sixty crab pots left onboard. It lifted the sorting table in the middle of the boat and then slammed it down with a loud bang.

She winced. Was it damaged? Anxiety coiled inside her. She couldn't afford the time to do a major repair. As a twenty-eight-year-old female rookie captain, she had a lot to prove.

She'd worked her tail off on fishing vessels ever since she was old enough to know she wasn't cut out for the traditional lifestyle of her Inuit ancestors, and realize that if she wanted to help her single mom make ends meet, fishing the Bering Strait was the Alaskan version of the lottery. The stakes were high as hell, but the potential for payoff kicked butt. Most days, Nolee understood the sea, and the mentality it took to work it. Today? She and the sea were not on the same page. At all. Making her wonder what she'd been thinking to talk her commercial fishing company, Dunham Seafoods, into letting her captain a ship of her own.

A picture of her large Alutiiq family, taped beside her radar, caught her eye. Her aunts, uncles and cousins goofed around for the camera, while her mother stood slightly apart, frowning.

Would her critical parent be proud of her?

"What's going on, Pete?" she called to her engineer.

The men had heaved the metal sorting table upright and Pete squatted beside it. "Wheel's broken."

Suddenly the bow dipped, and her eyes widened as a three-story wall of water rose and rose and rose in front of them.

"Take cover!" she screamed into the mic.

In an instant, the *Pacific Sun* bashed through a rogue, tsunami-sized wave, cleaving forward, plowing just below the surface, the world water. A deep shudder rattled through her and her breath was knocked clean out of her.

Reacting on instinct, she advanced the throttle, giving the ship more horsepower. They needed to bust through the wave. Not dive. She kept her hand steady on the controls, pleading with the sea to release her and her crew, and then they broke the surface, the gear scattered, her men gone.

"I need to hear from everyone, now!" she thundered, barely able to hear over the blood pounding against her eardrums.

Tyler crawled from between a couple of pot stacks waving an arm overhead, while the rest of the men staggered from their positions, clapping each other on the back, punching the air.

"It's getting squirrelly out there," she announced when she trusted her voice not to betray her concern. Crab fishing and coddling didn't mix. "Inside, guys."

Her men shook their heads and disappeared from view into the galley below. Just then a piercing alarm shrilled. She shot to her feet. The high water sensor!

Pete appeared on deck and sloshed through the rolling water to throw open the hatch down to the keel, Everett fast on his heels. A sickening bile rose in her throat.

Stu, her relief captain, raced up the wheelhouse stairs. "Leak?" he asked, his voice a gravelly smoker's rasp.

She nodded, then flipped on the speaker to the engine room. "Pete. Tell me what's going on."

The sound of rushing water crashed through the speaker.

There was static, and then Pete's faint voice emerged. "We've cracked the cooling pipe. Nine to ten inches."

"How much pressure is coming through there?" A rush of air escaped from between her clenched teeth.

"It's gushing." His gruff words were like hands on both her arms, giving her a shake.

She cleared her clogged throat, twice, then asked, "Can we replace it?"

"Yeah. But not out here. We don't have that piece."

The boat dropped several feet, rolled. "Rubber wrap won't hold it," she mused out loud, her pulse skyrocketing. Clamping down her panic, she turned the boat slightly to keep it from pitching so much.

"It's our only shot," came Pete's grim voice.

"All right. Use baling and wire it up good. Stop that leak."

"Roger."

After several minutes of battling growing swells, more alarms blared on-screen. Failed bilge pumps. Engine power loss.

No.

She blinked at the words and a dark shadow pressed at the base of her skull, rising. The possibility of the ship sinking seeped into her consciousness. Squeezed. Nearly drew blood.

She pressed her eyes shut for a moment. Gathered herself. "Stu, I'm heading out. Keep us afloat."

"Roger. Will do."

Grabbing her gloves, she clattered downstairs and donned waterproof gear. She blasted by the remaining hard-faced crew and scowled when they rose to follow her. "Stay put," she ordered, then listed, side to side, down the short hall to the portal and shoved down the latch.

Instantly, the wind snatched the door, swinging it wide and making her stumble, frigid spray buffeting her, knocking her sideways. Her boots skidded, and she crashed to one knee. Warm, iron-tasting blood washed across her bitten tongue.

She ignored the ache in her leg and pushed on, fighting her way to the engine room. Her breath came in short gasps that misted in the salty, water-logged air. After climbing down the wall ladder, she dropped into knee-deep flooding.

Pete labored over the cracked pipe. She shoved through the brackish swirl toward Everett and spotted three mostly submerged bilge pumps. A dark ring scorched their tops. They'd overheated. Beyond fixing. Her mouth vacuumed itself dry.

"Tell the guys to put on their life jackets if they're not on already and bucket this out while you replace those."

Everett frowned fiercely. "We've only got the one spare."

She swore under her breath. Not enough. Not even close. "Hook it up fast."

Everett grunted, then clambered topside.

She thought quickly. Without enough operating bilge pumps to stop the rising water, and the pipe still spraying, the engines wouldn't reboot, leaving the floundering *Pacific Sun* at the mercy of the relentless sea. Buckets wouldn't do much.

Still. She wouldn't quit. If she lost this eight-million-dollar boat on her first time at the wheel, she might never have another shot at captaining one and leading the independent life she'd worked hard to achieve.

But even more important, the safety of her men came first. They counted on her, as did their families. Even as another wave tilted the wet world sideways, sloshing frigid water past her knees, Nolee couldn't help thinking about them. Everett had a newborn son. Pete had postponed his honeymoon until the opilio crab season, which they'd gotten special permission to fish early, ended. They all needed this run.

She wouldn't let anything happen to them.

Back in the wheelhouse, she snatched up her radio, her eyes meeting Stu's. "Mayday, Mayday, Mayday. This is the vessel *Pacific Sun*. We're taking on water."

White noise crackled through the speaker. "Roger. *Pacific Sun*, this is United States Coast Guard, Kodiak, Alaska, communication station. Over."

She relayed rapid-fire specifics. "The seas are pounding us," she concluded, her voice hoarse. "Not sure how long before we capsize."

Speaking the words made it all the more real. She'd never been seasick a day in her life, but right now, she knew a whole lot about heartsick.

"Roger that. Jayhawk is on the way with ETA of twelve minutes. Swimmer and pumps will be deployed."

Bittersweet relief washed through her as she left Stu at the helm and joined the bucket line. On one hand, she didn't want to be rescued. Never had. But on her life's balance sheet, the US Coast Guard owed her big-time for the life-gutting sacrifice she'd made to them nine years ago when she'd given up the person who mattered most to her. They could damn well pay up with some help today.

She passed heavy pails among her crew, fighting a losing battle against water that wouldn't stop coming. Half the buckets spilled or sloshed most of their contents before making it over the rail, the deck pitching so fiercely below their feet they could barely maintain balance. She worked fiercely, doggedly, and thought she'd weep with relief when she finally glimpsed orange as the Jayhawk passed over the ship. Keeping her head down, she continued to pass slippery, frigid buckets until Tyler pointed out that the rescue swimmer was on his way down.

She stared up at the dangling rescue swimmer descending onto her bucking deck. The mountain-sized man, clad in a bright orange suit, unhooked himself and strode her way, his step sure and nimble despite the heaving boat.

She blinked, suddenly feeling more off-balance than ever, fooled into thinking she knew him. It was just the outfit. Just that cursed Coast Guard swagger. Yet there was something about the broad-shouldered shape, the assured step and the bone-deep confidence visible in the green eyes behind his clear mask as he drew closer.

It couldn't be.

"Dylan?"

He'd sworn never to come back to Alaska, had left without a goodbye. Her legs and arms went slack, and for a second she thought she might smack the ground.

The worst mistake of her life flipped up his visor. Spoke. "Hello, Nolee."

NOTHING IN PO1 Dylan Holt's military training had come close to preparing him for this.

He peered into Nolee Arnauyq's fierce brown eyes, recognition firing through him even as another swell sent him teetering sideways. Thick black hair dripped onto cheekbones that jutted so high and sharp her eyes turned to almond slivers. In the arctic air, Nolee's full lips trembled slightly, pale against tawny skin.

Someone he used to know; someone he damn well should have forgotten.

Right.

Get the job done, idiot. And get the hell out of here.

Kicking his ass into gear, he tore his gaze off her beautiful face and assessed the on-scene conditions. The *Pacific Sun* listed now to port at thirty degrees in high seas. Without propulsion, they could sink in minutes. No time to lose. He hoisted one of the two dewatering pumps dropped behind him on deck and turned back to Nolee. "Lead the way," he shouted over the rise and hiss of the sea, cursing his luck at being the swimmer on duty today.

He'd once promised himself he'd never see her again.

She nodded, hefted the other sixty-pound pump, and turned, as economical and tough as ever. Captain of her own ship, apparently, and how impressive was that? But then, he remembered well what it was like to crew with her on a fishing vessel. She never expected anyone to cut her any slack, an attitude that had always won over the crustiest of seadogs.

And it was no different on the *Pacific Sun*, he could tell, as she led him past a line of life-jacketed men passing buckets from the keel. She'd had the foresight to ensure they'd all geared up in preparation for the deadly waters. She'd protected them, but hadn't let them quit, either.

He and Nolee handed the carbon-monoxide-emitting pumps over to crew members to secure topside where they wouldn't endanger lives, and descended down into the engine room, unreeling the hoses to vacuum up the flooding. The whoosh of incoming water filled his ears.

Shit.

This looked worse than reported.

Water sprayed from a pipe that a man, standing in thigh-deep water, was attempting to wrap with rubber. Another fisherman secured what appeared to be a replacement pump, their movements clumsy in the arctic flood, their efforts futile given the size and pressure of the leak. The *Pacific Sun* was past the point of no return.

"We've got to abandon ship," Dylan shouted to Nolee.

She shoved back her hood and squinted up at him. Her dark eyes flashed, ink. "No!"

Damn that stubborn, reckless streak. Age hadn't tempered it. She was every bit the spitfire who'd rocked his world as his first love, the only woman to whom he'd ever given his heart. And he'd gotten it back in pieces.

"We've only got enough fuel for fifteen minutes on scene. I need to get you off this vessel."

Her mouth worked for a moment, and she peered at her laboring crew members. She nodded slowly, her expression inward, then shoved back her shoulders. "Get everyone to safety, but leave me be." She turned to the guys working on the pipe and pump. "Everett. Pete. Tell the crew they're abandoning ship."

"The hell we are," one of the guys swore.

"That's an order."

The man shook his head and dropped the wire into his pocket. "Roger." He and the other crewman climbed up and out.

Nolee squinted back at Dylan for a moment then held out a hand for the hoses. He cursed under his breath. He'd left her before, once, when she'd given him no choice, but history would not repeat itself today.

Not under these conditions.

Not a chance.

Still. She was a civilian and captain of the vessel; he couldn't compel her to follow his orders, much as he wished otherwise. After he got the crew off, he'd return for her and make her see reason.

"I'll be back," he vowed. He handed over the nozzle, snapped down his visor and headed topside. It took every ounce of will and training to leave her in the belly of the doomed ship. He'd learned to live his life without her, but that didn't stop his instinct to protect her at all costs from surging back to life.

On deck, the fishermen continued bailing as the guy Nolee had called Everett lugged the dewatering pumps' outtake lines to the rail and dropped them over the side of the unstable boat.

"6039 this is Holt," Dylan spoke into his headset. When a wave swelled off the port side, he grabbed an oblivious guy, a young kid barely out of high school by the looks of it, and scrambled for cover by the winch. Water buffeted them for several seconds as they huddled and then he tried again. "6039 do you copy?"

"6039 copy," his Jayhawk pilot and mission commander, LCDR Chris Abrams, said in the flat monotone they adopted in even the worst situations. "What's your onboard assessment? Over."

The wide-eyed teenager stared at him, his skin pale. When one of the men hollered, "Tyler!" he jumped to his feet then trudged back to the line.

Dylan stayed behind, listening hard. "They've got three feet of water in the hull and rising fast. Vessel is listing heavily. Structural integrity severely compromised with inadequate time to attempt repairs. We're abandoning ship. Basket requested. Over."

"Roger that," Chris said, his voice crisp. "Basket is being deployed."

Another oceanic blast tipped the vessel so that the rail drove to the surface before righting itself. He pictured Nolee below. He needed to get moving to return to her.

Inside his neoprene suit, his slick skin flushed hot, his blood humming with adrenaline. He emerged from cover and joined the crew who now held on to lines as the boat rose and dipped violently.

He cupped his hands around his mouth and hollered, "We're abandoning ship. Who's coming first?"

The fishermen eyed him, then one nudged an older crewmember forward. The man, with white hair and a craggy face, glared at him with red-rimmed eyes, uneven teeth bared between cracked, flaky lips. "I ain't going first." He pointed at the young guy in the blue slicker. "Take the kid."

"Right." Dylan nodded, understanding that it'd be a waste of time arguing with a sailor who'd rather risk losing his life than his pride. "Let's go."

For the next several minutes, Dylan toiled as the storm refused to lessen its grip, placing survivor after survivor into the basket until only he and Nolee remained on board.

"We have one minute," he heard his commander say through his helmet's speakers. "Is your captain ready? Over?"

"She will be," Dylan answered, his back teeth pressing together hard. He slung an arm over a rope line and held fast when another swell lifted him off his feet, dragging. The ship groaned as sheets of metal strained against each other like fault lines before an earthquake. The lashings clanked. "Send down the strop. Over."

Given the helo's low fuel state, he had barely enough time for the dangerous hypothermic double lift.

"You have fifty seconds and then I want you on deck, Holt," barked his commander. "Over."

The sea receded and Dylan shoved his way along the slick deck, propelling himself forward across its steep slant. "Roger that."

He would get Nolee out. End of story.

Descending as fast as he dared, he fought the wind and dropped down into the hull again. Icy water made his breath catch even with the benefit of the dry suit. Nolee should have been out of here long before now.

"I've almost got it." Her strained voice emerged from blue lips. Her movements were jerky as she twisted wire around the still gushing pipe.

His eardrums banged with his heartbeat.

She was losing motor function. Hypothermia was already setting in. With only thirty seconds left, he made an executive decision.

"It's over, Nolee. Come with me now."

He would haul her out by force if necessary. Braced himself for just that.

Yet when she opened her mouth, her head lolled. Her eyelids dropped. Reacting on instinct, he grabbed her limp form before she crumpled into the freezing water.

His throat closed, and he had to make himself breathe. He hauled her up and out of the hull and across the deck where a rescue strop dangled. Damn, damn, damn. His hands weren't cooperating, his own motor function feeling the effects of this cursed sea. Once he'd tethered them together, he gave his watching flight mechanic a thumbs-up for the hoist. The boat flung them sideways, careening over the rail.

Swinging, their feet skimmed the deadly swells. The line jerked them from harm and sped them up through the stinging air. He tightened his arms around her. Imagined them made of steel. With only a tether connecting her to him, he couldn't lose his grip. It was the difference between saving her life and causing her to fall to her death.

As they rose, he forced himself not to look at her. He'd dreamed about that face too many times, even after he left Kodiak to forget her.

But he wouldn't be doing his job if he didn't hold her close. And heaven help him—no matter how much she'd gutted him nine years ago—he couldn't deny she felt damned good in his arms.

2

NOLEE WAS LYING *on warm, gritty sand, water circling around her toes, breathing in the Alaskan summer fragrance of salt water and dense cedars. There was a delicious, decadent taste in her mouth—berries and chocolate, and possibly wine. She lifted her head and the afternoon sun glinted off the blue ocean so brightly, she had to squint through sparkles of light to see her feet in front of her.*

Her toenails were painted a deep rose. Girly and sweet. Not her style at all. And the nail polish had even been applied well. No smudged cuticles or bumpy surfaces. Someone was lying next to her, propped up on his side. Someone she cared about, who made her laugh, with big feet, nails unvarnished and clipped.

Dylan.

He stroked her bare stomach with a firm hand, the circular touch languid, deliberate, filling her with teasing heat, a pleasant ache beginning between her thighs.

Somewhere in the distance, gulls cried and the cool ocean thundered as it crashed ashore, swirling up and over her calves, then suctioning her skin as it receded. A throaty chuckle sounded beside her. She curved toward it, her body fitting against Dylan's instinctively, her toes curling in delight when his hand skimmed lower still, sliding along the edge of her bikini bottom.

"Nolee," he whispered in her ear and she tipped back her head at the rich sound of his voice.

"Dylan," she murmured, but could not be sure whether his name was flooding her thoughts or she had spoken it aloud.

"What are you thinking?"

She pressed her lips together. Stopped herself from revealing how she really felt and explaining why she'd been quiet on their summer outing. If Dylan left her, her heart would break, but he couldn't know that.

She started to say something flippant, and then he reached around to cup her ass, bringing her hips to his, the heat of him emanating through the thin nylon of his shorts. Her skin burned fiercely against his everywhere they touched, and she was incapable of speech, or of thinking anything at all. Shivering hunger took hold. She craved more.

Skimming her hands up the curves of his strong arm, she absorbed the tension of the muscles beneath his hot skin. She glanced at his handsome warrior face. Reached to trace the straight bridge of his nose, to touch the scar just above his arched right eyebrow and the tiny dimple in his square chin. She met his scorching green gaze. He had that way of looking at her. Intently. Passionately. With heated promise, as if he knew all of her erotic fantasies and intended to make each one come true.

It undid her.

He lowered his face. "You're driving me crazy," he whispered directly into her ear, his warm lips grazing the sensitive lobe.

"Me, too," she gasped as he continued stroking her,

slowly, tantalizingly, eliciting a lush heady response to his touch so that her heart clattered.

"Tell me what you want," he rasped, his voice an edgy growl.

"You," she groaned, a dizziness taking hold as her hand smoothed along his ridged abdomen. "I want you, Dylan. Always."

She felt him brush the hair back from her temples. His unsteady fingers conveyed the same need that licked through her.

"You're beautiful," he murmured, his voice insistent. Husky. Then he slid across her, inch by inch, like a tide, and she lay back so that she was flat on the sand, sinking into it.

In the sizzling afternoon, she could smell the sea on him, feel the faint grittiness of the salt on his skin as his muscular body shifted over hers, firm and solid. And then, she could feel his breath, the shocking, numbing firmness of his mouth a moment later as Dylan's lips melted into hers.

He kissed her, slowly and tenderly, his weight easing onto her so that she was overwhelmed with lust, the hardness of his body against her. His lips lingered and sampled. Tasted and nibbled. When his tongue glided over hers, the sensual contact triggered waves of pleasure that rippled to her toes. Her fingertips.

She nipped at his lightly bristled jaw, his ears, her fingers brushing over his dark, close-cropped curls. He cradled her head as his mouth whispered along the sensitive length of her neck. The delicious caress stopped at the birthmark at the base of her throat. Lingered. Nerve endings short-circuited, flash-bang, beneath her skin.

She couldn't possibly get enough of the feel of him.

"Dylan," she moaned, her voice loud in her ears.

"NOLEE," SHE HEARD him answer, his voice rising as if it were a question. Her lashes fluttered. Lifted. Dylan's face swam into focus. He peered down at her, his pupils dilated, the black blotting out most of the green. His face pale.

She reached for him, needing him to anchor her when she suddenly felt so loopy. The effect of their incredible sexual chemistry, she supposed. She drew his face close and pressed her lips to his again, inhaling his sweet breath, feeling the heat of his skin as he responded to her, kissing her deeply. Ardently.

Adrift on this blissful current, her lashes fell to her cheeks. She felt Dylan tunnel his fingers through her damp hair and its weight surprised her. Took her aback.

They hadn't gone swimming. Not yet. Or had they? Why couldn't she remember?

She caressed his smooth jaw.

Smooth.

Her fingers stilled.

Then she noticed something else that wasn't right. Something thick and heavy separated them.

A blanket. No. Blankets.

And the automated sound of beeping machines filled her ears, not the ocean, the salted air now smelling of antiseptic soap and disinfectant.

The dream or memory or whatever it was dissolved and vanished, like a reflection on water. Nolee's thoughts sharpened, and she willed herself to open her heavy eyes.

She was in a small white box of a room lying on an uncomfortable mattress.

A hospital.

Not on the beach.

Not on her boat, either, because…

A strangled noise escaped her and she shoved Dylan

in the chest, forceful enough to make him stumble back, hard realizations knocking through her.

…Because in this reality, Dylan no longer loved her.

"You!"

Dylan shoved his hands into the pockets of his olive-green flight suit and stared wordlessly at a furious Nolee. Sporadic bursts of noise filtered in from the corridor of Dutch Harbor's medical clinic. A squeaky wheel, and the aroma of roast chicken, heralded the delivery of the evening meal to the small unit's patients. Stale air hung as still and heavy as a tomb.

Why the hell had he just kissed her? He shouldn't have angled in so close when she'd called his name. Tempted himself.

And had she meant it when she'd said she wanted him? Granted she wasn't fully conscious…but she'd said *always*.

Not that he cared.

Shit. He cared.

He wanted her. The driving need to haul her back into his arms, feel the press of her lush curves through her thin hospital gown, thrummed inside. Made his stomach clench.

He drew in a ragged breath. Raked a hand over his hair. "I'll get the doctor."

"No!"

He halted at the door. Turned.

She leveraged herself up on her elbows and then sat up. The pallor of her skin alarmed him, and snapped him back to the bed where he gathered her small, rough hands in his.

"What are you doing here, kissing me? Why am *I* here?" In the room's quiet, her soft voice, always at odds with her tough words, slid around him like a caress.

Good questions, both. At least he had an answer for the second one. As for why he'd kissed her, frustratingly, he'd been as unable to resist her as ever. He should've left with his flight crew after dropping her here and enjoyed his upcoming time off after a long shift. But he hadn't been able to leave until he was assured of her recovery.

"You don't remember the boat?"

Beneath the flicker of humming fluorescent lights, her dark eyes sparked. "I fixed the leak…" Her words trailed off like the last air from a deflating balloon and confusion crossed her face. "Right?"

He shook his head. "You were too late."

She snatched her hands back. "No, I wasn't."

"You fainted. Hypothermia." He gestured to the thermal heating blankets that concealed her gorgeous shape, the feel of her body imprinted on his muscle memory as clearly as the last time they'd made love on Summer Bay beach, nine years ago.

Her teeth appeared on her bottom lip. Worried it. Black brows slanted toward the small proud nose he'd always found sexy. "So the boat…" She swallowed the last of her words. Hard.

"Gone."

She dropped her head in her hands. Moaned. It took everything in him not to gather her close and hold her as he had moments ago. Suddenly her lashes, thick and black, rose. She peered up at him. "My crew. Are they…?"

"Safe. Still pains in the ass, though. They're in the waiting room and refuse to leave until they hear you're okay." He bit back a rueful smile as he recalled the ongoing battle between the boisterous fishermen and the nurses threatening to toss them out. If not for his military credentials, and his persistence, he might not have been allowed back here, either.

"They're assholes. But they're *my* assholes," she said affectionately. She rolled her eyes at him, and in an instant their old connection slammed into him. He pictured the gritty young woman he'd worked alongside on his Uncle Bill's crab-fishing boat. They'd gone from friendly rivals to friends, and then much more.

What were they now?

He wouldn't stick around long enough to find out.

Her amused expression faded slightly, and she seemed to give herself a small shake. "Thank you for saving them."

He rested his hip on the narrow bed and fiddled with the green plastic hospital tag around her wrist, turning it over and over, unable to resist skimming his thumb along the satin flesh there. Her pulse jumped against his fingertip. "Not you?"

"I told you to leave me be." Her words escaped her in a breathy rush.

He caught and held her eye. "Not easy to do, Nolee."

Her nostrils flared, and the small diamond stud he'd given her when they'd graduated high school glinted. "That wasn't the case nine years ago."

"You think that was easy?" He strode out of the way of a food service worker bearing a dinner tray and breathed in the aroma of fresh-brewed coffee and chicken broth. Braced himself.

Get it together, man.

If you weren't in Kodiak, you wouldn't give her another thought.

Liar. If that were true, how the hell did he explain his nonstop thoughts of her over the years? The memories that refused to let him go, no matter how many miles he put between them. How hard he worked. The risks he took.

The squeak of the staff member's sneakers grew muffled and then disappeared. Dylan crossed his arms over his chest, willing himself to follow the cafeteria worker out and away from the tempting woman who messed with his hard-won peace of mind.

"Why are you here, Dylan?"

"Transfer." He turned to face her again. Knocked the emotion out of his voice. The hunger. Kept his tone crisp. "But it's temporary. I'm shipping stateside as soon as my out-of-rotation-year assignment request is approved."

"Of course you are." A bitter note entered her voice. She raised her chin and pinned him with a look. "How long have you been in Kodiak? Have you seen your parents? Bill?"

"Three months and no." He rocked back on his heels at her accusing expression. It wasn't like he was to blame for his decade-long family estrangement.

She dipped a spoon into her soup, eyes still on his, and lifted a steaming mouthful to her lips. When her sexy mouth pursed, he felt himself harden. "So they have no clue you're here."

He cleared his throat. Dragged his wild thoughts back under control. "Wouldn't make any difference if they did."

"For who? Your parents love you."

"They had a funny way of showing it."

"You know they couldn't help that. The business…"

"Was more important. Got it," he said, thinking of the wilderness expedition touring company they ran that'd overtaken their lives and overshadowed his childhood.

His older brother, Robbie, had taken to exploring rugged terrain like a mountain goat, his father had proudly proclaimed, praising their golden child at every opportunity. As for Dylan, after an unforgettable viewing of *The Guardian*, he'd known on the spot he wanted to be a rescue swimmer and travel the world helping those in need. He and his old man butted heads nonstop about his reluctance to toe the line in the family business, about his attitude, about the way he tied his shoes, the way he breathed… about anything it'd seemed.

After one blowout fight too many, they'd palmed him off on his uncle, who'd given him a place to stay during school and a job on his crab-fishing boat. Since they hadn't made one of his swim meets, missed his graduation, hell, just about everything, he'd decided to stop wasting his time missing parents he'd never really had and left Kodiak without another word when he'd gotten the call from the Coast Guard.

"That's not true," Nolee insisted. Her large extended family had always been a big part of her life. She'd never accepted his estrangement, a point of contention they'd had in their otherwise perfect relationship, along with her daredevil antics and unwillingness to leave Kodiak.

And her need to lock lips with his former best friend Craig.

He cleared his throat and his voice, when it emerged, sounded gruff. "Can I get you anything before I go?"

"A boat?"

One corner of her mouth lifted slightly, a grin-through-pain expression he'd glimpsed many times before. Nolee was the type to smile through a setback, laugh at an injury. It'd been the only way he'd known when she was really hurting. Despite everything, it bugged him that after growing up sleeping on family members' couches and in shelters with her health-challenged single mother, she'd finally gotten what she'd always wanted—a place to call her own—and he'd played a part in her losing it.

Then again, if she hadn't gambled on outrunning an unpredictable storm to take advantage of what he supposed had been an approved preseason run, she'd still have her boat.

Odds.

Nolee sure liked to play them. When she won, she won big, but when she lost…

He shoved the image of her sinking boat away. She was here now. Saved from her own worst instincts.

But who would be around to catch her the next time?

"Would you settle for Jell-O?" He pulled the clear wrap off the green, wiggling square on her tray. "And captain, huh? What you always wanted."

Her eyes searched his. "Why are you really here?" She gestured with a sweep of her hand to the room around them, frowning.

Because I needed to see your eyes open.

He squashed that thought, along with the temptation to climb into that bed and warm her up in a way that would be much more enjoyable for both of them.

"Professional courtesy."

She snorted. "My ass. Try again."

"Want me to call Craig? Maybe you'd rather have him?" he asked instead, then nearly bit his tongue off.

Her mouth dropped open. She stared at him for a moment in charged silence. "Get out."

He stepped forward, knowing he'd sounded like an ass, like the jilted boyfriend she'd turned him into, not the man who'd moved on with his life.

"Look, I'm…"

"You're what, Dylan? You saved me and my men. Thank you, but your mission is done and I don't need you anymore."

He hung his head for a moment, then lifted his eyes to search hers. "No. You never did."

Her gaze narrowed. Whatever she'd been about to say, however, was interrupted by a knock on the open door. A nurse bustled in and smiled at Nolee. "Ah. Good. Now I can tell your crew to hightail it out of here."

"Goodbye, Nolee." Dylan tipped his head to the nurse, cast a last look at Nolee and strode out the door.

Job done. Survivor's health ensured. Now he could get on with his day. His life. And get it back on track, starting with putting in his transfer request to leave Kodiak ASAP before thoughts of Nolee wrecked his head again. He'd moved on, damn it. Today was a minor setback. A brief reminder of what could have been. Nothing more.

Three hours later, after catching the ferry back to Air Station Kodiak, he hung from a diving board at his base's pool. He snapped off ten more pull-ups to complete his last set then let go, sinking to the bottom of the twenty-foot-deep end.

His body ached like he'd been hit by a truck and his chest burned. Sixty minutes of wind sprints, pull-ups and sit-ups. Another thirty jogging the track. An hour swimming. He should have exorcised his craving for Nolee by now. He gritted his teeth and pushed back against the instinct to surge to the top and drag air into his lungs. He stared up at the waving blue surface and envisioned the way she'd kissed him, her passionate response. She'd wanted him.

And he'd wanted her.

A swoosh sounded to his right as the shape of another service member plunged in beside him. Without missing a beat, the man shot him a quick middle finger then zipped to the surface, churning up the water with a lightning-fast crawl.

Anderson.

The newbie swimmer whose high-profile jeopardized mission three months ago had put the air station on alert and prompted them to assign Dylan to Kodiak to prevent more mishaps.

Sure. The commander had fed Dylan a line or two

to sweeten the raw deal he had no choice but to accept. Claimed they needed his expertise on these treacherous waters. Felt he could impart that knowledge to Anderson and rebuild the guy's shaken confidence. Promised they'd approve Dylan's transfer request after Anderson redeemed himself.

So now, three months in, the cocky FNG was interrupting his solo workout and challenging him? The hell with that.

Using his thigh muscles, he shot off after the greenhorn, his elbows jetting out of the water, his pointed fingers reaching, driving, cleaving through the pool. Feet and legs kicking powerfully behind him. His fatigue dropped away and he raced, pushing hard, until he caught up to Anderson on the third lap. They swam side by side for twenty minutes, then pulled up.

Anderson shook his head, sending droplets flying, and reached for the water bottle he'd left on the side of the pool. "Shit. Thought I had a chance of beating you since you'd been in here awhile."

"I was just warming up, asshole." Dylan drained the last of his own water.

"Heard about the *Pacific Sun*. Seven survivors." Anderson whistled. "And they have that hot female captain, right? Is she single?"

"No," Dylan said through his teeth. Nolee hadn't mentioned her relationship status and, of course, it was no damn business of his whether or not she'd stayed with Craig. But even in Anderson's wildest dreams, Nolee was out of his league.

"Hey!" Anderson threw out his hands as if to ward off the blow Dylan contemplated landing on him. "No offense."

"Just keep it professional," Dylan snapped, hating the

surge of possessiveness he had no right to feel. That damn kiss had kicked off all the wrong instincts in his brain. "How was patrol?"

Anderson hopped up on the side of the pool and dangled his legs in the water. "*Northern Lights* set a string in restricted waters. They were already correcting it when we came upon them. No excitement."

Dylan joined him and together they performed dips, lowering themselves, triceps flexing, into the pool, then pushing up again, and again. "You'll get plenty more once I'm gone," Dylan grunted as he repeated the move.

Now that Anderson was back in his fins with several successful rescues under his belt, and another swimmer had joined their SAR team as well, they could afford to approve Dylan's transfer request. Despite the promise from the higher-ups, however, he knew better than to count on it until he saw the damn thing.

"You have leave coming, right?" asked Anderson through gritted teeth, a vein appearing at his temple as he muscled through this set of twenty.

"A month. After that, I'm hoping I get a new assignment."

With this being an out-of-rotation-year move, he'd have to wait until a stateside RS position opened up.

"Can't say I'll miss you," Anderson said before disappearing beneath the surface and shooting along the bottom for the underwater swim portion of the workout.

"Me, neither," Dylan said to himself, thinking of Nolee, wondering if that were true.

Seeing her again messed with his mind, but she'd been right about one thing. He would seek out his family before he left Kodiak, just not the family she was thinking of. His parents had never had much use for him. His uncle, however, who'd nurtured his love of the sea, was on his list of people to see before he spent another decade away from Alaska. Dylan missed the old guy.

And, as an added benefit, spending a weekend with his uncle would ensure he wouldn't be tempted to cross paths with Nolee anytime soon.

3

"So you'll give me another chance?" Nolee leaned forward on one of The Outboard's pub tables the following evening, nearly toppling a couple of the empty beer bottles littering its sticky surface. Restless energy tap-danced in her veins. Made the balls of her feet bounce.

Rick Dunham, one of Dunham Seafoods's owners, signaled for another round, then shrugged.

"I'm considering it." He raised his voice above the din of the chattering crowd that filled the Kodiak dive favored by local fishermen. He popped a pretzel into his mouth and shot her an assessing look as he crunched. "These are the best quota numbers we've ever received and we need to fill them."

Over his shoulder, white lights blinked above a long, garland-wrapped bar where bearded men jockeyed for the best spot to watch the Seahawks game. A Christmas tree glowed red then green in the corner. Metal fishing lures dangled from its branches and reflected the light.

Rick's partner and younger brother, Sam, whistled. "Four hundred K. That's a lot of clams, eh?" He elbowed his brother. "Get it?" When Rick only glared at him, he continued. "But is she man enough for the job?"

"Of course," Nolee insisted, keeping her voice firm. Squashing her doubts. Captains didn't second-guess themselves. Her jaw was clenched so tightly it ached. She needed this to happen.

A waitress appeared and slid three dark ales across the table, foam sloshing down their sides. She pocketed the credit card Rick handed her, then hustled off.

"Fish and Game gave us special permission to start fishing preseason." Rick raised his glass and met Nolee's eyes over the brim. "Now that's wasted."

Regret bit deep, but she kept her face impassive. She tightened her grip around the cool glass to hide the slight tremble in her fingers and the exhaustion she felt after her close call. She hadn't expected the bout with hypothermia to take so much out of her, but she wasn't about to back down from a second chance.

Something too damn rare in her world. "*Pacific Dawn* needs a lot of work," Sam said, referring to another boat in their fleet. One in need of repairs, but possibly seaworthy with some elbow grease. He swiped foam off his moustache with the back of his hand while a cheer went up around a nearby pool table.

"I'm not afraid of hard work." She swigged back the malt. The smooth, mellow taste dissolved on her tongue. She blinked gritty eyes. Ordered her aching muscles to relax. Moments ago she'd expected an ass-chewing (which she'd gotten, understandably), followed by a kick out the door. Now she might have another shot at her dream. She wouldn't screw it up.

Rick gulped more beer, then lowered the half-drained drink to the table. "You'd need to bring her up to code before the regular season starts. That's only twelve days."

"No problem," she said with more confidence than she

felt, given she had no clue how much repairing the vessel needed. No matter what, she'd make it work.

Please give me this chance.

Sam jabbed a finger in her direction. "And we need that quota met."

As did she. Rick and Sam didn't need to spell out that her career was done if she mucked this up.

It was hard enough to become a captain, something she'd only done because Bill had taken her under his wing and taught her when he could. Yet even if she succeeded in getting to captain again, with a bad record she might have trouble getting a crew to sign on to work with her. She had to turn this around. No matter the odds, she had to take the gamble.

"I'll top those tanks."

"With crab this time, not water," guffawed Sam, cracking himself up. Suddenly his smile fell and his thick eyebrows knitted. "No more screwups. Our insurance might cover one lost boat. Not two."

A waitress bearing a steaming plate of chicken wings passed the table and dropped off their bill. Nolee's nose twitched at the spicy aroma. How long since she'd eaten? Slept? She was used to the punishing mental and physical demands of each crab season. But the anxiety that'd dogged her every thought since she'd woken in the clinic, minus one ship and plus several unwanted feelings for a certain swimmer, had taken its toll.

Rick signed the slip and pocketed his pen. The flat line of his mouth suggested he wasn't crazy about taking another chance on her. She'd be willing to bet he was hard-pressed to find another captain with any experience if he was willing to roll the dice with her.

"I'll get my crew and begin work tomorrow." She stood and extended a hand. Took charge of the situation. What did her Aunt Dai always tell her to do? Lean in? If she angled any farther, she'd topple over.

Her bosses shoved themselves to their feet. They exchanged a long look and then Rick grasped her hand. Pumped it up and down. "You've got yourself a boat."

"For now," Sam interjected, clapping her shoulder, sealing this last-ditch bargain she had to keep.

She grabbed her fleece off the back of her chair and yanked it on. At the far end of the bar, the live rock band swung into a guitar solo that squealed and whined, the sound blasting from wall-mounted speakers. Some of the milling plaid-and-jeans-clad men and women lifted their drinks and hooted. Their ball-cap-covered heads bobbed approval.

When a bouncer tossed a couple of tussling men outside, a gap appeared in the throng and Nolee's eye landed on Dylan, sitting in a dark corner across from his Uncle Bill. She glimpsed Dylan's chiseled jaw and noted his eye-popping body in a fitted green thermal shirt that she imagined did great things for his sexy eyes.

Buoyed by her win with the Dunham boys, she was on her feet and heading for Dylan before she had time to think it through. But she was drawn by the attraction that'd flared to life yesterday in a kiss she hadn't been able to stop thinking about.

She wove through the crowd just as Bill stood and pulled on a lopsided winter hat that looked to be the work of one of his six daughters. He never left port without having them sing him "Eye of the Tiger" for good luck and their drawings and pictures festooned his wheelhouse.

As she neared, she overheard Dylan saying, "I've got this."

"Hey, Captain Bill."

The older man looked up from zipping his coat and a broad smile creased his weathered face. "Nolee!"

Dylan's eyes swung to hers and the flare of heat in them made her pulse speed.

Bill engulfed her in a musk-scented bear hug that squeezed the breath out of her and lifted her off her feet. When he set her back down, she put a hand to her hair and felt Dylan's gaze. Her heart hammered in her chest.

"Heard about yesterday. Hell of a thing." Suddenly Bill jerked as if stung, and yanked a cell phone from his back pocket. He muttered under his breath then shoved it away. "Shoot. That's the wife again. Gotta go. Stop by *Easy Rider* when you can. Sure I can find some work for you."

Without waiting for an answer, he waved and disappeared through the crowd.

She spun a chair around backward, straddled it and beamed a full-blown cheeky grin meant to blast away the concern darkening Dylan's eyes. Pity. Growing up poor, powerless and dependent on others' charity, she'd had more than her share of it. She wouldn't let anyone feel sorry for her. Wouldn't let herself.

Besides, there was no denying it felt damn good to see Dylan. Seeing him in the hospital, feeling the old connection had melted away some of her reservations… And since he'd be leaving town soon, it was safe to bask in his sexy hot glow. She hoped. "You're off the hook."

The beginnings of a wry smile teased up one side of his gorgeous mouth. His shirt molded to his sculpted chest when he twisted around to search for a wallet. Her mouth watered. "How's that?" he asked without turning.

"Got another boat." She lifted the mostly empty tumbler in front of him. Sniffed. "So I've got the next round."

"You what?" He straightened and his eyebrows rose. In the dim light of the pub, shadows gave his symmetrical face dangerous angles that caught her eye. Turned the blood in her veins warm.

"Two Jim Beams, Sheryl," she called to an approaching waitress, forcing herself to look away. Act unaffected. She cracked open a peanut, tossed it in the air and caught it neatly in her mouth.

She needed to stop her runaway thoughts of Dylan. The devastating effect of his arousing kiss yesterday hadn't lessened. Not a bit. In fact, it'd seemed to intensify as she'd lain awake in her small apartment over her cousin's garage, staring at a neighbor's blinking Christmas lights, imagining him in bed beside her, distracting her troubling thoughts in the most erotic way possible.

And now that he sat only feet away from her, the effect was devastating. She couldn't stop staring at his hands. Recalling the strong feel of them on her yesterday in the clinic. His lips on hers. Electric. She'd thought the sensual side of her had died when he left Kodiak. But apparently he was the only man she'd met who could light that particular spark for her. Turned out, she'd missed it.

Warm, she stood and pulled off her fleece. When her head emerged, she caught Dylan staring at her, his eyes intent. His body still. Her jeans had ridden a little down her hip, revealing a small red-white-and-blue anchor tattoo.

"When'd you get that?" he asked, his voice hoarse. Without taking his eyes off it, he raised his glass and bolted back the rest of his drink.

"You like it?" She arched an eyebrow at him and sat again, enjoying the normally übercontrolled man's discomfort. Besides, it distracted him from any proceed-with-caution speech he looked like he'd been about to make. Tonight, riding high on her newly resuscitated career, she didn't want doom and gloom to rain on her parade. "I've got a couple more you might appreciate."

"I—I…" He swallowed hard, reminding her of that serious, earnest boy she'd met on Bill's boat who'd rarely spoken a word to anyone, who'd never smiled or joked around, but worked like a man possessed.

It'd become her mission to break his concentration back then, to make him laugh, get him riled, just feel something. Her daredevil antics had finally worn him down until he'd loosened up, then opened up, prompting her to lower her guard, too.

The old wound on her heart throbbed, a phantom pain, like a missing limb. It's not there, she reminded herself. Those feelings. Gone now. Poof.

"What's going on, Nolee?"

"Dunham Seafoods is giving me another boat." She tapped her fingers on the tabletop along to the beat of the band's Lynyrd Skynyrd cover and raised her chin a notch.

He frowned. "They just happen to have one they hadn't bothered putting out this year?"

She shrugged, looking as unconcerned as possible. "It needs a few repairs."

"How many?" he asked heavily.

"I don't know," she admitted, unable to hold out when he looked at her so directly.

He rubbed the back of his neck and gave her that squinty look she'd always found so sexy. "You have no idea how much work the boat needs to be seaworthy?"

She took a deep breath. "I'll know tomorrow when I inspect it."

"So you just accepted, sight unseen?"

"Yes." She stabbed the cherry in the bottom of Bill's glass with a toothpick.

"Why would you do that, Nolee?"

Sheryl returned with their drinks. At the shake of

Dylan's head, she trotted off with a quick wave, leaving Nolee's money on the table.

"Because I'm a captain minus a boat," Nolee insisted. "In case you forgot."

"How could I?" His eyes searched hers and she dropped her gaze, uncomfortable with all that worry. "Look, you could work for my uncle. Take a breather. Figure things out. You're a first-time captain. You shouldn't be taking a boat out unless it's been proven."

"I'll get it up to code." She raised her glass, refusing to let his worries get into her head when she had enough of her own. "Cheers."

"By when?" he asked, ignoring her toast. Placing his elbows on the table he leaned closer and his distinctive, clean male scent, a blend of soap and sea, sand and sun, rose around them. She breathed deep. After he'd left Kodiak, she'd fallen asleep clutching one of his old hoodies, her nose buried in the worn fabric, until eventually his smell had disappeared.

Not so her attraction, it seemed.

"The regular season starts in twelve days." He swirled his whiskey.

"I know," she said, firm, not letting his doubts burst her bubble. Or the tantalizing nearness of him sway her. "But I've got to fill my quota."

"What is it?" he asked, sounding wary. A throaty howl rose from the game-watching crowd at the bar, accompanied by a hail of insults for the Seahawks' opponents.

"Four hundred K."

Dylan leaned back in his chair, fiddling with the top of a leftover beer bottle. He shook his head. "That was taking into account the preseason. Your time's cut by a third."

"I'll make it."

"Be reasonable, Nolee. Who are you going to hire this late in the season?"

"My crew." Though, oddly, four of her six men hadn't returned her calls today when she'd checked in to see how they were doing.

"Bill told me he'd heard some of them got hired already. You know experienced hands are hard to come by."

She blinked at him, thoughts scrambling. "Oh." To cover her confusion, she gulped her drink and fought off a cough when the back of her throat caught fire.

"Right." He raised his voice when a pack of boisterous locals swarmed close to play darts. "You don't have enough help."

"I'll hire some."

One of the players landed a bull's-eye and a deafening roar erupted.

"This late in the season?" Dylan asked once the noise died down. "The only guys you'll get won't have much experience, or references. Going out to sea, this time of year, with a green crew, is suicide."

"Cod season's over." She drained her glass, needing the boost. "Some of those guys might be looking for work." Dylan had a point, not that she'd heed it. Catching fish instead of crab wasn't the same thing at all. Not even close.

"Why are you doing this? Taking these chances?"

She shrugged. "It's not chance when you know what you're doing." All the confidence she'd gained from her accomplishments filled every syllable, full and weighty. She wasn't the same woman he'd left nine years ago, not that he seemed to recognize that.

"You shouldn't have been out in that storm yesterday."

"Weather reports didn't predict it'd jog that far west."

"You gambled."

"To get ahead, you have to." Seeing him revert back to

the by-the-books, all-work-no-play guy bugged her. "You know, you and I aren't that different," she added, when he didn't speak. There was a brief silence. She looked at him, but was discomfited by the intensity of his gaze.

"What do you mean?" Their fingers brushed each other as they searched for unshelled peanuts in the bowl, the contact making her skin tingle in awareness.

"We both like living on the edge—we just went after that in different ways."

He stared at her for such a long moment, she wondered if he'd heard her. The crowd around the dart game swelled and a few pressed close to their table, jostling Dylan's elbow, making his drink slosh onto the surface.

He threw a couple of twenties on the table, stood and extended a hand.

"Let's go," he said. It was more a command then an invitation. Maybe his sense of humor had slipped lately, but not that air of authority, that strength that'd always drawn her. Challenged her. Turned her on.

She jammed on her knit cap, slipped a hand in his and let him lead her through the crowd, the group parting, making way for his broad-shouldered march. "Where?"

He paused at the door outside, lifted their hands and rubbed hers lightly against his chest, sending sizzles of excitement shooting through her. His voice deepened.

"Somewhere I can actually talk some sense into you."

OUTSIDE, THE CHILL shimmered off the frozen ground but did nothing to tamp down the heat Nolee's nearness stoked inside Dylan. Dressed in a blue fleece and faded jeans that outlined her delectable curves, and work boots that underscored her tough-girl persona, she drew his eye. Kept him looking as they tramped across the icy parking lot.

A ragged plume of air escaped him. Being this close

to her, alone, was playing with fire. He was having a hard time keeping his hands to himself. Yet he needed to make her see reason.

And satisfy the drumming hunger to have her to himself for a few moments, one last time, before he shipped out of Kodiak.

"My truck's over here."

Nolee spotted a red pickup that must be his, and she looked at him directly. The wind lifted and tossed long dark strands of her hair across her lips, luring his attention to their fullness, making him remember the soft feel of them against his yesterday. Driving him to want another taste.

"Okay."

A moment later they were seated on the plush seats, the ignition purring to life. Heat blasted from the vents and an old-school thrash band tune thumped in the dark, intimate space.

"I remember this song," Nolee mused, shooting him a sidelong glance.

When she rubbed her gloveless fingers together, he raised his hands to hers, touching them, and then, more firmly, enclosing them within his own. He brought them to his mouth and blew on them, unable to resist the impulses pounding through him.

Her liquid eyes rose to his and the challenge in them made his stomach muscles tighten, his whole body respond.

It took every ounce of strength to tamp down his desires and focus on what he'd brought her out here to say. What he needed her to hear.

"There's a difference between calculated risks and recklessness," he began. His voice emerged husky, low. She was so close he could feel her breath. Her body was rigid, listening, her fingers now laced in his. Her cool skin was blistering.

"We both like putting everything on the line. Admit it." Her mischievous smile kicked up his heart rate by several blood-pounding notches. She smelled like an ocean sunrise and he breathed deep.

"Not true." He lowered their joined hands to her lap. She was wrong. He wasn't the wild risk-taker his parents saw him as—she really was that way, not him.

"Come on," she scoffed in that tone that'd always called him on his bullshit. "Remember the time we jumped from Jagged Rock Falls? You took my dare."

He nodded mutely, recalling that twenty-foot leap into churning waters, her body pressed to his afterward, behind the roaring falls. The material of his jeans tightened around his swelling groin. "I could never say no to you."

He brushed a thumb along her knuckles and a visible shiver passed over her skin.

"You should have," she whispered against his cheek, straight into his ear. His whole body hummed with unleashed hunger for her, not heeding the warning reminder in her words when he damn well should have. He forced himself to let go of her hand.

The music shuffled to another one-hit wonder hair band tune and she tensed beside him. "Is this the…"

He gritted his teeth to keep the telling admission from escaping. Then she snapped her fingers beneath his nose and shot him a knowing look. "It's the playlist I made for you for your nineteenth birthday. Why are you still listening to this?"

"Some things have a way of sticking with you."

The teasing look in her eyes faded and she blinked a little too swiftly before she dropped her gaze.

They sat in silence for a moment and he stared out the windshield at the point where the black sea met the sky.

"You didn't object when I dared you to jump in our ice fishing hole, either," she said after a moment.

"We nearly froze to death."

"We warmed each other up," she countered.

The buzz of blood in his veins at that wicked memory seemed to throb along to the thumping beat. "We made good use of that fishing shack."

He caught the quirk of her lips in the gloom. "Though we didn't catch a single fish. Not that we cared."

No. He'd only cared about Nolee back then. Had insisted, over her objections, that he would give up everything, his dreams of joining the Coast Guard, of leaving Kodiak, because she'd been what mattered most.

And she hadn't felt the same way.

The windshield began to fog and he flipped the heater to defrost. A couple of snowmobiles whined in the distance and a memory resurfaced. "We stole that ski-doo." He felt himself smile at that crazy day that'd nearly landed them in the ER and jail.

"Borrowed," she clarified, shifting, her knee bumping his. He was aware of the press of her against his side, hip to hip, leg to leg, arm to arm.

"We didn't have permission."

She sighed. "The real crime was Mr. Strout never riding the damn thing. Plus, I didn't hear you complaining when you did donuts with it. You had us going fifty miles an hour."

"That was kid stuff. This is real life."

"Exactly, Dylan. It's my life. I call the shots in it. Only me."

"You came way too close to losing it yesterday," he growled.

She reached a hand to his cheek. Laid her palm flat against it. His breath lodged in his chest and his mind went blank. "But I didn't."

No. He was acutely aware of just how alive she was here beside him, short-circuiting his brain. His defenses against her were running low. God knew, he was trying his damnedest to do the right thing and save her from her worst instincts before he left Kodiak.

"What if you hadn't been rescued in time?"

"Then I would have died doing what I love. Isn't your motto So Others May Live?"

"That's different."

"Is it?" She angled her head and her dark eyes met his in the dimness.

"I risk my life to save other people's lives. You're risking yours for profit."

"You're wrong."

"Then what?" He stroked a hand through her mane of straight, glossy black hair, the strands running through his fingers like a silken waterfall, her eyes closing in pleasure.

"I want to be independent. Free," she murmured.

He watched her breath quicken and he felt the barrier he'd erected between them start to crumble.

"We've both always wanted that," she added.

Something inside him shifted. Loosened. "Nolee. I don't want anything happening to you."

She raised her face, lips parted, as if in a question, and put her hand to the scar above his brow, tracing it with her fingertips. "The worst thing that could happen to me is nothing."

He groaned at the brush of her mouth against his jaw. In an instant he had her in his arms, his heart pounding against hers. It was only a few seconds, but it was as much as a man on the edge could take. He stripped the hat from her head and tossed it on the dashboard, while his lips descended to hers.

And he kissed her with all the longing that had been plaguing him since he'd laid eyes on her again.

4

DYLAN KISSED NOLEE with a hunger as fierce and edgy as her own. She'd waited so long for this—this man. This night. She'd dreamed of it. Fantasized. Practically wished upon a freaking star…a star that would lead him back north to her. But how long would he stay?

She shoved aside the troubling thought, wanting to focus only on him, on this moment. His touch woke her dormant body, tingling and aware with a stinging, rushing need. For the first time in ages, she was warm. More than warm. Heat burned through her, chasing away the cold.

He slid from behind the wheel toward her and she threw her knee across his lap and straddled him, the move automatic, her body remembering him instinctively. She felt his familiar, well-muscled legs against her thighs and the long hard length of his erection. Her mind grew foggy from passion and desire, chasing away coherent thought. Right now, all she knew was that she wanted to be close to him, held by him.

Dylan threaded his hands through her hair and met her eyes for one blistering-hot second, his gaze raking over her intently. Her heart pounded at his sexy perusal. It seemed as if his guard had been stripped away and the emotion remaining was something frightening and thrilling at the same time.

"So damn sexy," he breathed, his voice hoarse. Fervent.

Then his mouth landed on hers again and she forgot to think. His kiss teased her with a hungry quality that robbed her of reason so that she could do nothing but cling to Dylan's broad shoulders. Covering her lips with his, he tasted her with the confidence of a man who knew her. Knew what turned her on, what drove her crazy. What left her overwhelmed and powerless with lust.

She savored the familiar way their mouths merged and melded, the heat intensifying with each stroke of his tongue as he teased his way inside. Tipping her head back, he exerted more pressure over the kiss, the effect drugging her. Then he cupped her cheeks, angling her face to kiss harder, deeper.

A light-headed sensation spun the world around Nolee and she wrapped her arms around his neck, holding on tight. Her fingers combed through the short curls at the base of his scalp. Soft, she thought hazily. Thick.

Her breath stuck in her throat and she sat utterly still when Dylan released her hair to run his hands down her sides. In one swift move, he freed her jeans' front closure. Then he cupped her bottom, fitting her to his groin. Sweet, hot, delicious friction. She nearly groaned aloud, desire building, air now hissing between her teeth. He edged her low-riding denim down her hips slightly, the warm air teasing her skin, making her ultra-aware of the tiny patch of flesh he'd just bared.

The purring vent was no match for the fogged windows that insulated them, making this intense moment private. Intimate. The hard, thumping rock song that poured from the sound system pounded along with her erratic pulse.

Her fingers grasped ineffectually at his jacket zipper,

her hands incapable of making progress when his kisses consumed her. His hands stroked a hot path up her rib cage to palm her breasts through her coat, then spanned her ribs with his fingers. She arched against him and whimpered, a keening sound that didn't begin to express the desperation now clawing inside. When her fleece provided a soft, thick barrier to his touch, he slid it off her body with hands now clumsy, shaking with the same hunger that gripped her. An electric current within sizzled double-time. It ignited a fire low in her belly.

He delved deeper into her mouth as his kisses turned more deliciously aggressive. The wicked intent she sensed behind the wet mating of mouths thrilled her on a primal level, stripping away the need for anything other than raw, scorching sex that would leave them both gasping for breath.

She tugged down his jacket zipper at last, needing to feel his body against hers, his hot, naked muscles against her hypersensitive skin. With fumbling touches, nerves buzzing, she eased it open and he shrugged out of it, his magnificent chest rising and falling against the thin thermal fabric of his shirt, their ragged breaths mingling. Fast. Urgent.

She wanted every erotic act she knew he had to offer, and she wanted it now. She wiggled her hips against him to be sure he knew how much. His primal growl rolled right through her, strengthening her determination to simply enjoy the searing chemistry between them for as long as it lasted.

Hoots and hollers erupted in the distance as customers exited the pub. An engine fired to life and then headlights whisked across the space before disappearing, tires spinning through icy snow.

Alone again, she melted into his arms, collapsing

against him, her hips grinding with more urgency. The warmth between her legs made her damp with want. He swept her hair to one side and his lips traced the side of her neck, then the hollow of her throat. Their breaths came shorter and then shorter still. Beneath his rapidly rising and falling chest, his heart thundered along with hers.

Thick, steamy air settled on her bare midriff as he slid up the hem of her shirt. Never one to bother with a bra unless strictly necessary, Nolee delighted in Dylan's string of appreciative oaths as he discovered that fact with his hands.

"You're mine," he breathed, just as he cupped her breasts fully, taking the weight of her aching flesh in his hands. Her breath seized in her chest at his possessive declaration. Oh how that was true.

Every atom of her being fired to his touch as if he held the key to turning her on, to winding her up this way. With slow deliberation he dragged his thumbs over both taut peaks. She practically convulsed with the sharp contraction of her feminine muscles when he tweaked them between his thumb and forefinger, at the same time nipping her lower lip between his teeth.

His rock-hard thighs beneath her only added to the spiraling heat. The equally solid length of his arousal gave her no quarter in that direction, either. Not that she wanted any. His body provided an erotic cradle for her hips, along with the growing knowledge things were only going to get hotter.

Nolee broke the kiss so she could simply look at the man in front of her. She touched his face, tracing a fingertip over his lips, up one cheekbone and then down. She smoothed the scar above his eyebrow and part of her relaxed. This was Dylan. He wasn't a stranger but a familiar lover. A man her heart recognized, craved, dreamed of more often than not.

Looking at him now, it was as if she was seeing him for the first time all over again—the stinging rush of attraction, the need to glimpse his smile, the desire to hear his laughter and, even more, to be responsible for it.

Above all, though, was the yearning to touch him. So she did. She traced her fingers over the indents that defined each ab, each contracting, rock-solid plate, and he caught her fingers before they settled on his bulging groin.

Her lashes lifted and she peered up at him, the fog of desire unraveling slightly at the edges. His sculpted features swam into focus. They looked sharp enough to cut someone. A muscle jumped in his clenched jaw.

He ran a shaking hand over his short brown curls. When he spoke, each word emerged heavily. "I hope I'm not stepping on Craig's toes here."

She stopped breathing for one suspended minute. "Craig?" Her strangled voice shoved past her heart, which had leaped into the base of her throat and lodged there.

He stared at her gravely with unblinking eyes. "Craig."

"You—you think I would kiss you like that if I was with another guy?"

His anguished eyes delved into hers. "You know why I might think that."

His quiet words fired through her. They reminded her of her anger when he'd caught his friend manhandling her and had jumped to conclusions. Dylan always assumed the worst. Given his critical parents' abandonment, she understood why he would expect life's letdowns. Back then, she'd been naive, thinking she was the exception from that view. Stupid to think the years might have changed him.

Clearly, he was the same person. And so was she. It was

the reminder she needed to steer clear of him. To be glad he'd be transferring from Kodiak soon.

"If you think that about me," she said through shaking lips, "then you don't know me at all."

She threw off the hand he'd placed on her wrist, yanked down her shirt, flung open the truck door and hopped out, her fleece shoved under her arm.

"Nolee!"

She whirled. "What?"

"Tell me you're not taking out that boat."

"Why wouldn't I?"

"Have you heard the weather predictions? They're expecting record-breaking temperatures. Storms."

"So?"

"You'd be a fool to go."

"Yep. That's me." She studied his familiar, handsome face then turned and spoke over her shoulder. "Always the fool."

THE FOLLOWING EVENING, Nolee stretched her aching muscles. She'd spent the day retrofitting the *Pacific Dawn*'s crab pots for opilio and now dutifully stood behind a table laden with a variety of modern and traditional Alutiiq dishes, serving their community during the annual winter festival. The air was thick with smoke, fresh seafood and the occasional curse. Her stomach growled and she sighed with relief at the dwindling end of the buffet line.

"Do you want an extra scoop?" she asked as she ladled soup into a stooped man's outstretched bowl. He shook his head and smiled, his skin exploding into lines that radiated from his eyes and mouth.

"That is enough."

She nodded and rubbed her low back. She needed rest. A hot soak to relax her screaming muscles. And an aspirin.

Her brain hurt worse than her body. Her spirit? Flatlining. The *Pacific Dawn* needed more repairs than she'd imagined. With only eleven days left until inspection and the opening day of the regular season, she wasn't sure she and her remaining crew members would have the boat seaworthy in time. To fill the impossible quota she'd promised her skeptical bosses, she couldn't miss even one day of the regular opilio season.

Making matters worse, she couldn't stop thinking about Dylan. Last night's kiss had shaken loose feelings she needed to keep locked down. It'd felt so right, so perfect to be in Dylan's arms she'd almost forgotten all of the very solid reasons things hadn't worked nine years ago. She'd made the right choice to let him go then, and she needed to steer clear now and focus on her career and her family.

"Take a break." Her Aunt Dai squeezed her arm and nodded in Nolee's mother's direction. Kathy Arnauyq sat at the end of a long folding table that had been mostly cleared by hustling volunteers. She was small, dark and intensely serious, her gray-streaked hair in a braid she'd pulled forward over her right shoulder. A young couple and their three boisterous children occupied the opposite end. "It's time you talked."

Nolee bit back her sigh. Since losing her boat, she hadn't dared visit her mother, unwilling to subject herself to a solid round of I-told-you-so's. Tonight, though, she couldn't put it off any longer.

The chair scraped against the tiled floor when she pulled it out and seated herself opposite her parent. "Hi, Mother."

Kathy nodded as she toyed with the metal spoon in her empty coffee cup. Her neat, slightly sharpened features revealed none of the discomfort twitching through Nolee.

"Did you get enough to eat? Because I could—" She

cut herself off at the shake of her mother's head. "Okay. What would you like?"

"I'd like you to leave the Bering Sea and come back to Kodiak. Stop this foolishness," Kathy said in the feather-soft voice that made others lean close and pay attention.

Old frustration flared inside. "Captaining a boat is not foolish."

"A commercial boat." Kathy's hands were cool as she pushed a lock of hair away from Nolee's eyes in a tender gesture that nearly brought her to tears. "They're greedy. Taking more of the world than is needed. That's not our way."

Nolee sighed. "No. It's not." She'd grown up being taught the value of subsistence living, a part of her tribal culture that went back thousands of years. What others might consider poverty, they believed to be a revered, responsible way of living. For Nolee, however, it'd been a relentless childhood of scraping by on whatever family members could toss their way. Their poverty had made them powerless, her mother's precarious health preventing her from holding down a lasting job. "But I need to pay the bills. And where is your oxygen tank?"

"It broke." Her mother lifted a hand in greeting as a very pregnant woman shuffled by, her hand pressed to the small of her back, a child hoisted on one hip, another clinging to the hem of her long shirt.

"Broke?" Nolee nodded to another of her cousins then turned back to her parent. "Is it getting repaired? Why didn't anyone tell me?"

Kathy wheezed. "I don't want to bother you. Your Uncle Mak will help when he gets back from his truck route."

"I'm getting it repaired," Nolee said, her voice firm.

"With what money? You've lost your job. Now you'll come home to me."

"Home? And where's that?" The frustration of her mother not understanding Nolee's choices roiled in her gut, souring each word, the taste so bitter she was sure that if she stuck out her tongue it'd be yellow. "Whose house are you living in now?"

Kathy's hurt expression filled Nolee with shame. "Why is a building important? We're surrounded with love. Family. That's what matters."

Her mother had a point, but somehow it'd never been enough for Nolee. Growing up, every part of her life had been so entwined with others in her extended family that she'd gone out of her way to establish her own identity, one that wasn't so dependent on charity. Someday, she'd have enough savings to buy her mother a house and lift her from the abject poverty that kept her sleeping on family members' couches. Especially now that her bad health, with her chronic obstructive pulmonary disease and her diabetes, was deteriorating further. "Not for me."

Kathy reached out and covered Nolee's drumming fingers. "No, my restless spirit, you are your father's daughter."

Nolee stiffened. Her white father had disappeared once he'd gotten "itchy feet," according to family whispers, abandoning her and her mother when she was just an infant because he'd been bored. That—that was selfish. Not like her. She would never turn her back on her loved ones the way he had.

The way Dylan had...

"I'm nothing like him," Nolee blurted out, stung. Growing up mixed race, she'd always felt as though she straddled two worlds, slightly off-balance, never sure where she truly belonged. Only Dylan had taken the time to really know her, to push and challenge her as an equal, someone worthy of respect.

Her mother took her glasses off and cleaned them with the cloth of her shirt. "Yes. More than you think. He was independent, too. Didn't want to rely on anyone but himself."

"I—I—" Nolee struggled to answer an accusation that hit home. Needing others was a weakness, and she'd always striven to be strong. "He left because he didn't love us, Mom."

After sliding on her eyewear, Kathy peered at Nolee. "You can't open your heart to love when you won't depend on others."

Nolee squeezed the bridge of her nose hard between her thumb and forefinger. It felt like there was a band of pressure squeezing tightly around her skull, her thoughts knotting.

If love meant relying on someone else, someone who'd probably let you down, leave, hurt you, then she wanted no part of it. The feel of Dylan's arms around her returned, as did his passionate kiss, the memory as tender as a fresh bruise. She needed to stop pressing on it to see if it still hurt. Time to switch the heavy topic.

"I've got another boat."

Her mother's nostrils flared. "How?"

"My bosses have a big quota they need filled so they're giving me another shot." Nolee observed a woman at the next table, snapping irritably at a little boy. Nolee wrinkled her nose at him over the edge of her glass to try and make him feel better. He stared back at her, seemingly stunned, then broke into a toothless grin.

"They're taking too much crab." Kathy's angled eyebrows lowered until they met. "Wasting."

"There's a market for them. Supply and demand." Nolee stared into her mother's unrelenting face, then softened.

She would fulfill her family obligations, even if her mother didn't feel she needed the help. "Forget it."

"The land and sea don't belong to you."

"I know," Nolee interrupted, all too familiar with the saying. "We belong to it. Why do you think I still live here?"

"That's not why you're still in Alaska, Nolee."

Kathy's all-knowing gaze leveled on her and Nolee dropped her eyes to the table, flustered. What other reason could there be? Her bone-deep connection to Kodiak kept her rooted here in her Inuit world. It had been the reason she and Dylan hadn't worked out. Right?

Suddenly, her mom's breathing grew labored and Nolee rushed around the table to her, concern rising. She shouldn't have pushed things. Nolee's mother had done her best. Now it was her turn to do what was right, even if her mother didn't approve of her methods.

"I'll get you a replacement oxygen tank tonight and stop in to visit before I leave next week. After that, I'll only be able to call when I come to port to empty the tanks."

Kathy inclined her head and a stream of light shone in her piercing eyes. "Take only what you need."

Nolee nodded.

Her mother was right. Respecting the world, others, herself, meant taking only what she needed.

And the aggravating feelings that'd risen for Dylan yesterday were definitely not what she needed right now.

Not one bit.

He made her wonder if she was the island she'd always tried to be, complete and happily solitary…especially when he'd just highlighted the hole in her heart.

5

DYLAN LEAPED ABOARD *Easy Rider* and strode past the wire crab pots stacked twenty feet high in preparation for next week's launch. A light morning fog rolled in from the harbor, shrouding the view. Above, gulls wheeled and dived, their cries muffled by the mist.

Despite having the entire preseason to ready the boat, Uncle Bill's deck buzzed with last-minute activity. Deckhands tested lines, repaired equipment and brought bait aboard, the headless cod carcasses dangling to their knees, the strong, briny smell curdling the air. Nervous anticipation hung like sea mist over the docks.

How was Nolee faring? He tried shoving his concern aside but it lodged as deep as the feelings for Nolee that'd been clamoring since their kiss. Getting her out of his mind, his thoughts—hell, his fantasies—was impossible. Every time he closed his eyes since their hot hookup two nights ago, he saw her flushed, passionate face. The wicked, teasing smile she had bestowed on him in the truck. Her hungry eyes that had reflected his own pounding need for her. The soft, lush feel of her against him.

And she'd accused him of not knowing her when he'd asked about Craig…

Him? Not know her?

He knew every part…at least he had…right up until she'd cheated on him with Craig.

"Hey, Dylan," a voice called through the boat's PA system.

He wheeled around, then peered up at the pilothouse. Behind the glass his uncle waved. "Permission to come aboard, sir?" he called, only half joking. Captain Bill ran a tight ship.

"Too late for that," his uncle boomed. "Get your ass up here before I put it to work."

The crew joined in a collective laugh as Dylan pulled open the wheelhouse door and jogged upstairs. Inside, Uncle Bill swiveled around in a cracked, black leather captain's chair. On three sides of him blinked electronic gadgets that reminded Dylan of a Jayhawk cockpit. The stale scent of cigarettes rose from an overflowing ashtray next to the throttle.

Dylan tossed a grease-stained paper bag at his uncle and threw himself into another seat. "Just fried."

Uncle Bill's face lit up. "Ah, you shouldn't have." He pulled out a handful of fries then offered some to Dylan.

Dylan shook his head. "So. Why'd you ask me over?"

"Sure as hell wasn't to see that ugly mug of yours," guffawed Bill, his phlegmatic laugh ending in a short coughing fit, his belly jumping beneath an oversize Seahawks T-shirt. Chomping, he pulled down a gooseneck mic and spoke into it.

"Sullivan! I ain't paying you to sleep. Break's over!" he barked, then leaned back in his seat. "Should've never agreed to take a greenhorn this year. Nothing but a liability. Those guys don't know how to work."

"He'll learn," Dylan assured him, thinking of himself and Nolee. They'd been just sixteen when they'd met aboard his uncle's ship as newbies. He pictured her small, ferocious face as she'd crawled inside pots to bait them. Her lightning speed at sorting crab. Her daring, won't-quit attitude that had dragged him from the dark place he'd inhabited back then. He couldn't have gotten through any of it without her.

"Or he won't, and I'll have to toss him overboard," Uncle Bill growled with the grumpy good humor that kept his jumping crew seesawing between laughter and terror. "Anyways," his uncle continued, pointing a limp fry at him before shoving it into his mouth. "Ran into your mother in town. Mentioned you were here. She wants to see you."

Dylan stiffened. "Why?"

Bill chewed slowly and studied Dylan. "She misses you."

A short laugh escaped Dylan. "That'd be a first."

"Your parents did their best."

"Well, their best sucked."

"Maybe she wants a chance to make it up to you."

Dylan frowned. If so, then it was too little too late. "They made their priorities clear, and I wasn't one of them."

"People can change, Dylan."

"Not that much."

His mind leapfrogged back to his rigid, oppressive childhood, the survivalist drills his hypercritical father forced them through, day after day after day, the competitions where he'd pit Dylan against his much-bigger brother, every piece of their lives held tight in his ruthless grip.

What are you? A little girl? he could hear his father taunt from outside a dirt-drawn wrestling circle. *Competition makes you tough.*

Then, *Jesus, don't cry, Dylan. He's your older brother. Did you think he'd just let you win?*

Or, *Take it like a man.* Cementing for Dylan that he'd never be the kind of man his father wanted him to be.

Later, his mother. *Sweetheart. Your father means well. Can't you try a little harder to get along? He's only doing this to make you stronger. You have to be tough to live here in Alaska.*

That's when Dylan had vowed to leave Kodiak one day and never look back.

There was no point in reconnecting with people who'd only made him feel lousy about himself.

"Just consider seeing her before you leave Kodiak."

"I don't—"

Uncle Bill cut him off with a swat of one of his massive hands. "I said think about it. That's all."

Dylan blew out a long breath. "Fine. I'll consider it." Which he wouldn't, but he couldn't argue outright with the only person who'd ever cared about him, growing up.

A tall, redheaded man on deck caught his eye. "Hey. Isn't that Everett? Nolee's deck boss?"

The pop-fizz of a soda tab opening sounded. "Yeah," his uncle answered after a long gulp. "Good man. Came here looking for a job after she lost her boat."

"Well, she's got another one." A growl had entered Dylan's voice and his stomach muscles clenched.

"Which one?"

"The *Pacific Dawn.* Guess it needs repairs."

Uncle Bill choked on his drink and set it down. "The damn thing hasn't been at sea in over fifteen years. She'll need months of work."

"Tell that to Nolee. She's planning on fishing with it in a week."

The squealing grind of metal on metal sounded below, and Dylan glanced out the window. A shower of red sparks colored the gray day as a welder crouched beside the launcher. Had Nolee scheduled her inspection yet? Once she had a full evaluation, would she finally see sense?

"Nuts."

"Yeah. And you've got to tell her so."

Uncle Bill laughed in a grunt and shook his head. "Son, haven't you figured out that you don't tell that gal what to do? She's got a hard head."

"You're the only one she'll listen to. Who can talk her out of it."

"Nah. I trust her." Captain Bill took a long swig of his soda, and then he continued, "Nolee won't take her out unless she thinks she's worthy."

"We're talking about the same Nolee, right?" She'd always been reckless. Impulsive. Had that prompted her kiss last night? She'd gone from passionate to stone-cold when he'd stopped to verify her status with Craig. It was clear she was no longer seeing the dude, so why had she gotten offended about his question? Was it guilt over past actions? He shoved his balled hands into his pockets.

"She's changed," Uncle Bill mumbled around another bite of fries.

"Not from what I've seen," Dylan grumbled, thinking of her refusal to abandon a sinking ship.

"She's a hell of a captain," avowed his uncle with a finality that shook some of Dylan's convictions. "Wouldn't have taken her under my wing if I'd thought she didn't have what it takes. It's a certain kind of person that can captain a ship. Not everyone can do it, but Nolee...she's a natural. She deserves this chance."

"To kill herself and her crew? The weather this season..."

"Looks like a bear." Uncle Bill tossed out his empty bag and stuck an unlit cigarette in his mouth. "Seen the predictions but it ain't gonna stop me or any of the rest of us, including Nolee." He held a lighter against it until the end glowed red. After a couple of quick puffs, he said, "And I ain't about to try and stop her. In fact, I'll help her out when I can."

"She won't take it."

"Nope." A long stream of acrid smoke accompanied the word. "She never does. Still, I'll offer. She's spent these past nine years laboring harder than any man I've ever worked with." Captain Bill waved the cigarette clamped between his thick fingers. "For a girl with her humble beginnings, it's damn impressive what she's achieved. She worked her way up the ranks, proved herself to the crew and even our bosses. You should respect that, son. I sure as hell do."

At a shout from below, Uncle Bill turned to his mic and began a rapid-fire exchange full of cussing and directions. Then more swearing. Dylan stared out the window at the veiled world and pictured Nolee somewhere in it, laboring, striving to make her way.

Uncle Bill had a point. Nolee's humble beginnings made her deserving. Stubborn. She'd never back down. Not when she had legit reasons to want this and not a lot to lose. Her life, he realized, wasn't half as precious to her as it was to him.

Again he recalled their childhood struggles, how they'd confided in each other, vowed not to let their upbringings define them. This was Nolee's dream just as much as the Coast Guard was his.

He shoved himself to his feet and pulled on his wool cap. "I'm heading out. Good luck out there."

A red-faced Uncle Bill slid him a sideways glance, his blue eyes barely visible beneath the heavy hang of his brow. "Luck ain't any part of it. It's all skill."

Dylan pointed at the horseshoe nailed above the exit door. "Keep telling yourself that."

His uncle's deep chuckle followed him out the door. He strode across the deck, leaped onto the dock and headed out in search of Nolee's slip. Deep down, they all knew luck had a lot more to do with it than anything else. Skill and sound equipment couldn't always save your ass. Especially in a catastrophe.

But it paid to hedge your bets. Be prepared. Like the Coast Guard's motto, Semper Paratus. Always Ready. That was something Nolee couldn't achieve on her own when she was short on crew and time. He could help her with the equipment part of things. Size up the *Pacific Dawn*. Determine the extent of the repairs for himself. Now that he'd gotten the newbie rescue swimmer up to speed, he had time off coming—one month leave.

It was the least he could do. His duty. His time in the Coast Guard had taught him never to turn his back on those in need of help. It was a mindset too ingrained for him to deny. Yes, he should keep his distance, but he wanted to ensure she had a viable boat before she embarked in the growingly rough winter seas. Besides, those sizzling moments in his truck had ignited old feelings he needed resolved.

He'd missed some things about Kodiak after all, and spending the day on a boat beside Nolee was one of them. He hoped he could uncover her mysterious response to him. It shouldn't matter, but it did. It didn't affect his plans to leave Kodiak. He wouldn't get emotionally involved with her again, but at least he'd get closure on the events that had changed the whole course of his life.

He passed small and large fishing boats, the freezing temperature turning his breath into white exclamations of air. Seagulls hovered on invisible currents overhead in the clearing sky. A pair of pelicans, farther out to sea, folded their wings and dove into the gray chop. In the distance, the white-capped mountains loomed over the dramatic landscape that drummed a beat inside him he hadn't heard in a long while. It spurred his feet. Lengthened his stride so that in minutes he'd reached a tall black boat.

Pacific Dawn, he mouthed, reading the gold script lettered on the side. He craned his neck and appraised the large vessel. About a hundred and twenty feet or so, he assessed, bigger than Nolee's last. Older, too, considering the dated equipment. He spied Nolee, sprawled on top of a twenty-five-foot crab pot stack wearing her bulky fleece over fitted jeans, doggedly repairing a hole in its netting, her beautiful face flushed beet red, from what he could tell at a distance.

He stomped up the gangway and her head snapped up; thick dark hair hung in her beautiful face. His body tightened as his gaze dropped to her full mouth.

"What are you doing here?"

Good question. One he didn't have an easy answer for, so he went with the truth. Or as much as he'd admit.

"Saving your ass."

"My ass is just fine, thanks."

He eyed the sexy curve visible from her prone position.

"Indeed, it is," he drawled and gave in to a full-on, appreciative smile that lifted the corners of his lips and made her almond eyes narrow.

He clambered onto another pot and set to work when she pointed her chin at a stack and returned to tying up loose netting.

Would he be able to work close to her and resist the attraction? It would be hard, but he wanted her to succeed. Maybe if he helped her with this, he'd feel satisfied she'd be okay, and then he'd be able to walk away again…this time without regrets.

His gaze slid over her sexy shape and his pulse pounded along with the hammering crew on deck.

Yeah.

Well.

Good luck with that.

6

NOLEE PEERED DOWN at the paper in her hand late the following afternoon and her gut twisted. The dock's pounding mix of sound, the muffled clang of metal against metal, the whine of a cutting instrument, receded, giving way to the rush of blood in her ears. "All of these safety modifications need to be made?"

"At a minimum." Dylan loomed huge and solid beside her, his arm brushing her shoulder. She breathed deep and strove to settle her jumping heartbeat. Working beside Dylan for the past day and a half had kept her on high alert, her body humming with sexual tension, her eyes drawn to his long, lithe form as he effortlessly scaled masts, leaped atop pot stacks and muscled through lifting and positioning equipment, working tirelessly to help her.

Should she have accepted his offer?

She'd been determined to banish Dylan from her mind, and then he'd suddenly shown up to help as if their devastating kiss had never happened. With her challenges mounting, she'd had to agree.

She released a ragged breath and focused. Or tried to, with so much lean muscle in close proximity.

"On top of repairs…" Her gaze drifted over the boat and

stopped on Tyler, her gangly greenhorn, as he repaired broken decking. At the snail's pace he worked, she'd be lucky if he finished even one of his assignments in the nine days before their departure date. He slammed down a hammer, then screamed and held his thumb to his mouth.

"Want your mommy?" catcalled Flint, her other returned crewmember. The garrulous, elderly seaman worked faster than Tyler. She needed four more of him, and she'd had only three responses to the ads she'd posted around town. She stifled a groan.

"Back to work!" Nolee called, refusing to give in to the impulse to baby Tyler. Who hadn't worked through a bruised finger…or a broken one? Crew needed toughness. Not mothering.

Dylan's thick-lashed green eyes bored into hers. Behind his left shoulder, the sun was setting. It sank toward the horizon, orange bleeding into gray-blue. A cargo ship was silhouetted black against the dramatic sky.

"The Coast Guard will board you at some point. They'll force you to return to port and disrupt your fishing." He wore an off-white cable-knit sweater that accentuated his defined chest and slim waist, and jeans that hugged his powerful thighs and tight ass, making it impossible for Nolee to stop her eyes from drifting over him. Sticking to him like wallpaper.

"Do you accept bribes?" On impulse, she trailed a finger down the shifting musculature of his abdomen and felt his stomach muscles contract beneath the wool. Damn, he felt good.

He sucked in a fast breath. His large hand closed around hers and rubbed it against his iron chest. Beneath her palm, his heart thudded. His eyes burned into hers.

"Don't play with me, Nolee," he growled, his voice deepening to a whole other level of sexy.

"Who's playing?" she joked, her voice catching slightly at the end, her knees weakening at the hot expression in his eyes that made them glitter and darken. He could turn her to liquid caramel with just one look.

"Captain?" called Flint. She forced herself to tug her hand loose and turn to her crew. "Tyler here says it's time for his animal crackers. Can he knock off?"

She studied a woebegone Tyler. He thrust his gloved hands inside a large Carhartt jacket that hung on his thin frame, and shifted on his feet. "Only if you say so, Captain," he mumbled.

How long had they been working straight? She peered up at the faint glimmer of a star in the darkening periwinkle sky. They'd arrived at dawn and hadn't stopped, working at a blistering pace that hadn't made much of a dent in her list. Despair rose and she squashed it fast. Somehow she had to make this work. She eyed the mostly vanished sun and let out a breath. "Go ahead and knock off."

The men raised and lowered their chins as they ambled off the *Pacific Dawn*, calling good-night, joining other fishermen hustling to The Outboard. The smell of something frying drifted up on the arctic air, sharp and gingery. Trout, she thought. The bar's Friday-night special.

Dylan stepped close once they were alone. In an instant, Nolee became acutely conscious of the sexy stubble he'd let grow on his square jaw, that heady clean, male scent of his that got her pulse picking up speed. "Ready to quit?"

Understanding the double meaning in his question, she raised her chin. Met him square in the eye. "Hardly. I'm interviewing possible crew members tonight."

He angled his handsome head and peered down at her. "How many have you got?"

"Lots," she said breezily, stepping down the gangway. Dylan caught up to her in three strides. He cupped her elbow to steer her past a man wheeling a stack of bait and she jerked away, the feel of his touch lingering. If anything, it spread, permeating her coat's fleece as if it wasn't even there and triggering every last one of her body's responses.

"So—what—ten?" he asked. A brief silence when she didn't respond. "Five?"

She slid him a sideways glance. Dylan. Good looks *and* brains. He never missed a damn thing.

"Three," she admitted, keeping her face expression-less in her best imitation of her mother. If only she felt this serene.

"Three?" Dylan exclaimed. He whistled. "We'll be lucky if they know how to swim."

When they reached the wooden steps to The Outboard, he snatched open the door before she reached the handle and ushered her inside. "They better be good." That husky rumble in her ear made her shiver in awareness.

"I'll let you know," she said as coolly as possible given the feverish state his proximity had put her in. There was something about the man that made her brain go haywire, made her lose her hard-won calm, cool and collected outer shell.

"No need." Dylan grabbed a seat at the only empty table in the bustling establishment. At the bar, hunched fishermen swapped tales and gobbled down the Friday-night fish fry with greasy fingers. A mic squealed over the speakers as a four-man band set up in the corner. The humid air swarmed with the stale smell of sweat and beer and cigarettes. "I'm staying for the show."

She crossed her arms and tried not to let that striking face of his disarm her. "I've got this."

He nudged a chair from the table toward her with the steel toe of his work boot. "I don't doubt it. Especially since, with three applicants and four openings, you're not in a position to say no."

"You're not going anywhere, are you?"

"Naaahh," he drawled, the corners of that sexy mouth curving up in a devilish way that made her want to laugh or kiss him or both. She licked her lips. Probably both. "Not for the next three weeks, anyway," he added.

She startled. "What do you mean?"

"Consider me your fourth applicant."

Her gaze drifted to that sexy grin of his that wouldn't quit. "And what position do you want?"

His eyebrow quirked. "Good question. Might be hard to choose." He stared up at her with a heat that had her knees melting out from under her. "But for now, let's start with deck boss. Everett's working with Captain Bill. None of the applicants will have that level of experience. Someone has to train the newbies."

"You said taking the *Pacific Dawn* out was dangerous. Foolish," she hedged.

"It is. Which is why you need me."

She did need him, damn it. As much as she wanted to flat out refuse him, she couldn't. And deep down, after spending this time with Dylan, she had to admit she wanted to see as much of him as possible before he left Kodiak again.

She opened her mouth and closed it, struggling to articulate her snarled thoughts.

"I believe a *Thank-you*, or a *You're hired*, will work."

"You really are annoying." Damn, he was gorgeous, with that pirate smile and those gleaming emerald eyes. That unforgettable face that sent her heart rate skittering.

"One of my best qualities."

"Fine. You're hired," she barked, dredging up her best captain's voice in an effort to sound more commanding.

In control. Of course, it only made his grin broaden into a full-on smirk. Infuriating man. How would she ever manage him? Manage the strong attraction pounding through her? "But not a word while I'm interviewing."

"Aye-aye." He rose to his great height and snapped off a precise military salute, his eyes twinkling roguishly. His tall, angular silhouette made her breath catch, his frame so strong and dominant. Yep. He was getting to her again. Shoot.

Now they'd be stuck on board together. Bumping into each other at every turn…how would she resist him?

She growled in frustration and flung herself down in the worn wooden seat.

"Two Jim Beams," he ordered when a waitress paused at their table. She blinked into his mischievous face, that slayer smile of his doing its work again, the woman rendered speechless.

"Straight," Nolee added, her voice a little strident. Dylan raised an eyebrow at her, looking amused, and the waitress jerked into action, whisking off a couple of beer bottles and plunking down a basket of peanuts before she hustled away with their order.

"Jealous?"

"Please," she scoffed, shelling a peanut and tossing the meat into her mouth, her narrowed eyes on their waitress, who now giggled with another server by the bar, looking their way. She wondered about how many women Dylan had been with since he'd left Kodiak and a spike of undeniable jealousy pierced her. Damn that swimmer. They'd been each other's first and since him, no one else had come close to turning her body to dust the way he had. She'd been relieved that he'd halted things in the truck. Now she wondered if it would be so wrong to bed him before he left? If she kept her heart out of it…

The door opened slightly and a small, twenty-something-year-old slid inside the bar, his movements ginger, his shoulders forward and diffident.

He had a hardcover book tucked under one arm of his tweed peacoat, which would have fit better on some Ivy League campus than in this rough-and-tumble dive bar. From his spotless wool cap to his polished dress shoes, he screamed outsider…not a status that went over so well at The Outboard.

When he accidentally bumped into a man at a pool table, the group paused in their game, lifting their heads one by one like a pack of hyenas scenting a lone baby gazelle. They quickly surrounded the outsider, who swiveled his head from one to the other, his pronounced Adam's apple bobbing.

"Hey. What have we here…" rasped one with a belly three times bigger than his small, close-shaved head. The bar had fallen silent as most of the patrons quieted and gawked at the developing spectacle.

Nolee noticed an intent Dylan out of the corner of her eye. His fingers dug into the edge of the table and he perched on the end of his chair, poised to leap into action. His lips were pressed into a grim line, his features hard. She recognized that I'm-going-to-kick-your-ass tough-guy expression, and a sense of comradeship began to build. They'd never shied away from bar brawls to defend themselves when they'd been the newbies on the fishing scene, and had looked out for others when they could. She exchanged a swift glance with Dylan and nodded. Some things never changed.

"If you're looking for the library, this ain't it." One of the men guffawed, pointing at the book.

"Thanks for that incredibly valuable advice," the man said in a crisp accent. "If you'll excuse me…"

His step forward was blocked when a third man pushed in front of him wearing a shark's smile. "Are you making fun of us, fancy pants?"

"Not at all. I hardly believe you'd be capable of understanding my humor, let alone be offended by it."

There was the briefest silence, then an outburst of cat-calling and whistling from the bar crowd. Nolee's mouth dropped open. Had she just heard him right…and did he have a death wish?

Dylan's mouth quirked.

"Huh?" exclaimed the bald sailor, looking at his befuddled buddies' faces as they shifted from one foot to the other, scratching heads of hair still stiff with salt water.

"Now. Step aside."

"Not so fast." One of the men, a former classmate of Nolee and Dylan's named Ted, shoved the book from under the newcomer's arm. It landed on the wet floor with a thunk. "Ya dropped something."

Dylan's chair scraped back and he propelled himself toward the group, Nolee fast on his heels.

Go time.

"Pick up the book, Ted," Dylan growled. The bristling sailor stepped back, alarmed eyes rising to meet Dylan's.

"Now!" barked Nolee. Her hard gaze met Dylan's and something warm exploded in her chest at his firm, approving nod.

"Oh. Uh. Sure," Ted stammered. When he swooped down to grab it, the stranger's foot pinned Ted's hand to the ground.

Nolee gaped as Ted tried and failed to jerk it free. "Come on, man. Let me up."

The other guys exchanged swift looks but didn't come to their buddy's aid.

"I believe you should apologize," observed the stranger coolly, sounding serene. Unruffled.

"Seriously?" Ted gasped.

"Yes."

"Fine. I'm sorry."

"I don't believe I heard that…"

"I'm sorry!" Ted hollered.

"Well. No need to shout," drawled the daring man.

The bar erupted in laughter and Dylan quickly steered the stranger to their table.

"Thanks for that," he said, sweeping off his hat to reveal a shocking mass of red frizz. "Wesley Cornelius Pryce." He thrust a hand in their direction and Nolee shook it, her body going still as recognition of the name swept through her.

"I'm looking for Captain Arnauyq."

Dylan angled his head, shot Nolee a sidelong glance and asked, "Why's that?"

"I believe she's seeking an engineer."

7

"THANKS, BUD," Dylan said to the bartender a few hours later, pocketing the keys he'd accidentally left behind. After walking Nolee back to her apartment, he'd realized they were missing and returned to The Outboard, where only a few diehards remained. The loss turned out to be a lucky break, considering how sorely tempted he'd been to kiss Nolee senseless at the door and carry her upstairs to satisfy the need that'd drummed through him all night.

He considered himself damn near a saint for keeping his thoughts to himself and heading back to the bar.

The way she'd handled herself today, working with her crew, then here in the bar—she had a body that would catch any guy's eye and serious guts to tough it out in a man's world. And the way she'd been looking at him tonight…she'd had him ready to back her into the nearest dark corner.

"Holt?"

Dylan swung around and pulled up short. Craig Winters. The last person he'd wanted to see in Kodiak besides his folks. The warm flirtation he'd had going on with Nolee all night dissolved as the memory of Craig kissing her rose hard and dark in his mind.

"Thought that was you. Don't know anyone else that size who doesn't play pro ball. How are you, buddy? Let me buy you a beer?" Craig leaned over too far on the brass-rimmed bar and toppled sideways.

Dylan caught him and helped the stumbling man back up, then shoved his balled fists into his pockets to stop himself from swinging them. That stuff should all be water under the bridge…especially since it was pretty clear Craig and Nolee must not be dating anymore.

"Later, Winters."

"Hold up! I'm leaving, too," huffed Craig. A hectic shade of red flamed his cheeks and the tip of his nose.

Dylan swore under his breath. "You're not driving."

"How else am I getting back to my hotel? Wife kicked me out last night." His eyes grew wet, and he snuffled loudly.

"Coffee," Dylan called to the bartender wearily, holding up two fingers. "Black." Much as he hated the guy, he couldn't turn his back on him. He waited for Craig to seat himself. It took a couple of tries.

"So. I heard you and Nolee are working together, eh?" Craig asked. The bartender returned with two steaming mugs.

"Drink your coffee, Craig."

"Right. Sure." He slurped down a mouthful then coughed, waving a hand in front of his face. "Oh. Hot. Anyways. Heard about you and Nolee. Back together again. Never thought you two should've broken up."

"No?" Dylan loomed closer and Craig angled back, nearly toppling off his stool again. "You had a damn funny way of showing it."

"Hey. That was my bad. Should never have kissed her like that."

"Like what?"

"By surprise. Uninvited."

Shock socked Dylan straight in the jaw. He rubbed it, his mind reeling.

"She never wanted anything to do with me then, and she's avoided me ever since."

Nolee's words returned to him. She'd accused him of not knowing her. Regret raged through him, dark and swift. She was right. He hadn't understood a damn thing.

"Look. I should've contacted you to clear things up. But you were so mad… And then you left town, and—anyway, no excuses. You deserved an explanation. I was a coward."

"Yeah," Dylan murmured, mind racing. So Nolee hadn't kissed Craig on purpose. The realization that he'd been wrong all this time about Nolee betraying him swamped him. Why didn't she tell him? Why the hell had she not set him straight?

After telling the bartender to call Craig a cab, he headed for the door.

Only one way to find out.

Ten minutes later, Dylan laid on the doorbell to Nolee's apartment a second time. Then a third. Finally, he heard her footsteps tramping down the staircase from her above-garage apartment.

When she flung open the ground-level door, his body went rigid at the sight of her. Heavy lids drooped over liquid brown eyes. Sleep-messed hair tangled around her beautiful, flushed face. He could no more keep his eyes from roaming down the length of her than he could stop his next breath.

A chill wind swirled around them and molded the worn material of her hip-length T-shirt to her curves, revealing the jut of her nipples and the dark circle of her areolas. He dug his fingernails into his palms to keep from reaching for her right there in the open doorway, his blood firing.

"Dylan?"

"We need to talk." His voice, when it emerged, sounded thick and rough, edged with the hunger blooming in his gut.

"Can't it wait?" She angled her head and her hair slipped over her shoulder and down her back, revealing smooth golden flesh where the cutout collar had slipped. He swallowed hard and cursed himself for coming here on impulse. He should have approached her on the boat, surrounded by crew, loud machinery, things to distract him from the greedy want that seized him.

"Not any longer," he insisted, his words stumbling over his swelling tongue. "I just ran into Craig. The guy you let me think you kissed. I need to know what really happened, Nolee."

The color drained from her face, and her mouth opened and closed. "Come in," she breathed after a moment, then turned and led him up the stairs.

Her ass cheeks, firm and round, bounced beneath the rising hem of her shirt with each step, and he felt himself grow even more aroused. His groin tightened and he sucked in a harsh breath at the jet wash of desire flooding him.

Concentrate, Holt. Time to get some answers. If he'd known the truth about that kiss, how different his life would be. He'd never have left Nolee. Or Kodiak.

The words shuffled then repeated in his brain.

You never would have left Kodiak.

Before he could fully process the thought, her fingers twined with his. She led him across the threshold into an unlit space and stopped in front of a large bed covered in a shoved-back quilt and patterned pillows. It dominated a cluttered single room furnished with an armchair in the corner, heaped with books, and a television atop a tall wooden bureau. A glow from the holiday lights on the house across the street streamed in a nearby window, washing the area in tones of muted color. He glimpsed a small galley kitchen at the far end and a digital clock on the microwave read two.

A rising storm rattled the windowpanes. White curtains of sleet began to fall. In the distance, a foghorn wailed as it sent fingers of light groping across the harbor. A sand truck ground past in the wet dark.

He dropped Nolee's hand and stepped back, needing to get his bearings. The warmth of her body made him breathe sharply. Her fragrance was exactly the same as he remembered. A heady mix of fresh sea air, salt-scrubbed skin, floral and musk. He gritted his teeth. Clamped down his rising desire.

Focus on your mission.

Compartmentalize.

"Why didn't you tell me the truth about Craig?"

She drew in a deep breath. Dylan's eyes fixated on the rise and fall of her breasts beneath the thin material of her nightshirt. He wanted to lean down and pull that teasing nipple into his mouth but kept himself in check. Barely.

"Let me take your coat," she deflected, drawing close.

Heat blasted through him as she reached out her hands, fumbling with the zipper of his jacket before she eased it down a few inches, just enough to expose his chest.

A growling sigh wrenched up his throat at the feel of her fingers spread across his shirt. The look she sent him as she lowered the rest of his zipper seared across him like a sunburn. He shrugged out of the jacket and let it drop to the hardwood floor. It took everything in him to keep from stripping off the rest of his clothes. And hers.

"Tell me what happened," he said, forcing the words past the desire clogging his throat. The nearness of her soft body captivated him, rooting him to the floor so that he couldn't walk away even if he wanted to.

Nolee's hand landed on his chest again, inflaming his desire, which was already riding the slippery edge of control. "There isn't anything more to tell," she said. Her fingertips grazed his abs. Their featherweight touch caused his skin to tighten as his muscles tensed. If she was trying to distract him, it was working, damn it.

Why was she dodging his questions?

What was she hiding?

She'd pushed him away when he'd asked about Craig the other night. Now she drove him senseless, evading him in a different way. Yet he couldn't ignore her or the all-consuming sexual attraction that crackled in the air between them.

He smoothed his hands over her shoulders, cupping the satin flesh. *Just for a moment,* he told himself. *Then I'll let her go.* His mouth found the edge of her jaw and nibbled. His hands tightened on her hips, pulling her into the cradle of his body.

"I want you," she mumbled against his mouth, her hips twitching between his legs.

"What?" He blinked through the fog of lust and saw her white teeth flash in a smile. He couldn't remember his name anymore, let alone what he'd come here to talk about.

She nipped his lower lip with a damp bite. "You heard me."

He met her gaze and what he saw there shifted the ground out from under him faster than any sea-washed deck.

No teasing. No flirtation. Just the same unadulterated passion, the same fierce need that blasted through him. She wanted him. And he wanted her.

Suddenly, she dropped to the edge of the bed. Her

T-shirt rode up, revealing an expanse of tawny, smooth leg, causing his adrenaline to surge, his heart to chug the way it did before he leaped into rough seas. Before he could respond, Nolee slid a hand up his thigh, slowly caressing the muscles there, stopping just short of his now straining erection. Heavy desire flooded his veins.

"Nolee," he rasped as she lowered the zipper of his jeans and reached for him, tracing a path down the front of his shaft with two silky fingers.

The fire he'd been suppressing inside him threatened to consume him whole. It was a struggle to fight against the urges pounding in his brain. Resisting her was a losing battle. His noble reasons for doing so began slipping away, receding, taking with them the last of his resistance.

"Oh, Nolee." Holy hell, that felt good.

"Shhhh," she whispered, her breath warm against his groin as she eased down his pants. After he'd kicked them off, she bent over him, her hair brushing his thighs. "Talk later."

And then her lips were on him, slowly mouthing his damp tip, and he lost his train of thought. His mind, too, as her tongue darted out and flicked the head of his cock, circled. Her eyes rolled up to meet his, her mouth suckling with excruciating slowness. She was driving him crazy.

Fuck it, he thought, *I can't fight this*. He threaded his hands in her dark tangle of hair and tugged her down, urging her to take more of him in. Then her mouth completely engulfed him. Slick and urgent. A jolt of hot pleasure sizzled through him, and with a groan, he feasted his eyes on the erotic sight of Nolee's plump lips gliding over him. Her tongue ran rogue up and down his length, dragging a deep growl from his throat, while she palmed his buttocks, squeezing.

He tipped his head back and closed his eyes, shuddering as she repeated that deliberate, wet glide, again and again, until he was mindless. The undiluted sensation of her soft lips and tongue brought him closer and closer to an incredible brink. He held off coming by sheer will, but each erotic draw of her mouth, each long lick, each flick of her tongue pushed him closer to the edge. But when he went over, he wanted her to be with him. Wanted to feel all of her wrapped around him. Wanted to watch her come.

He had to move her before she tempted him past the point of no return.

"Nolee." Her name was a plea for mercy, his muscles so taut he could scarcely move. "Sweetheart, you need to—"

He almost didn't make it, but she paused just then to peer up at him and see what he wanted. That reprieve saved him. Just.

He hauled her up against his body and his mouth landed on hers with none of the teasing skills he used with other women. This kiss was hot and out of control, his tongue stroking hers with unrestrained hunger as he eased her down onto the rumpled quilt. Clumsy with need, he slid her shirt up and over her head before he yanked off his clothes and tossed them into a corner. Then he pulled up short at the sight of her naked, delectable frame.

Wow.

She'd leveraged herself up on her elbows and the view of her, lean and curvy, ripped the air from his lungs. Froze his body then torched it an instant later.

Full breasts, round and firm, rode high on her slender torso. A delicate waist flared out into slim hips that made his mouth flood. His best memory of her couldn't do justice to the temptress in front of him. He reached for her long before he'd looked his fill. Nolee whimpered as he dipped his hand into her panties.

"Your turn," he whispered before brushing past the

silky fine hair to cup her mound, absorbing her feminine heat. She was wet and ready for him, leaving his fingers slick. He brought one digit to his mouth for a taste. The scent of her arousal drove his hunger higher.

She groaned low in her throat and her whole body strained toward him, her back arching, her breasts lifting, her hips thrust more fully against his hand. The appealing sound was earthy and animalistic, like a call only he could respond to.

Her voice nudged up an octave when he slipped one finger inside her to find the source of her heat. Slick and wet, she squeezed him even as she welcomed him, her body going limp as she sank into his touch, trembling. His every muscle flexed, hardened, strained to be a part of her, to get inside her and soak up all of that silky warmth.

"Dylan," she breathed, full throated, her eyes glazed and unfocused.

The sight of her, undone, her control gone, her body quivering just for him, filled him with deep masculine pride and a ferocious possessiveness.

He wanted to make her scream just for him. To take her places no one else could. A damn selfish thought for a guy who had no plans to stay in Kodiak and be the kind of man Nolee deserved.

More than anything, he wanted to share that bone-deep, earth-shattering connection and release only she had ever been able to get from him. The fierceness of that need gripped him with a force he couldn't deny. He would give her everything he could tonight, though not nearly all he wanted with so much still holding him back.

Not even close.

8

NOLEE SANK HER fingers deeper into Dylan's broad shoulders, realizing she'd made a huge mistake in using her body to distract him from his question about Craig. Now things had gone too far for her to stop.

Or to want to.

Not when his touch burned her clean through, her blood surging, clamoring need filling her. He was cupping her tingling breasts in his hands and low moans flew from her. When he rolled one nipple between his thumb and forefinger, the pleasure knifed straight through her to swirl low in her abdomen.

She felt her body tightening up inside, knew the signs of an orgasm waiting to happen. If she gave herself to him so completely, would she ever get herself back?

"Dylan, wait—" she began, desperate to slow this runaway train she'd stoked to life. Or at least seize back control. He'd turned the tables on her, and she needed to command this moment. It was barreling ahead without her knowing which direction it might take.

He rubbed the black triangle of her panties with two teasing fingers until Nolee thought she'd jump right out of her skin. "I want us to—"

He kissed the rest of the words away and paused the gentle massage that had her flailing on the edge.

"You first." He pressed his thumb against the throbbing center of her, no doubt feeling the racing pulse of that tender spot. "I can't wait to taste you again."

His words nearly undid her. If he hadn't removed the exquisite pressure of his thumb, she would have tumbled right over the edge.

Wrapping her legs around his body, she kept him close, craving the release that only he had ever given her. Her thoughts grew scattered. Even speaking took an enormous amount of effort. She could only feel, her every nerve tightly attuned to Dylan's touch. With every inhale she drank in more of the scent of his skin. The whiskey-tinged aroma of his breath.

When he slid her panties off, the rasp of his harsh intake of air filled her ears. She didn't think it was possible for the tension to coil any more intensely inside her, but at his intimate stare, her body responded with more heat. More hunger. More all-consuming need. A terrifying, exhilarating tide of powerlessness surged through her, pulling her under, sending her spinning. Tumbling.

When his gaze finally met hers, there was something dark and possessive flickering in his eyes. "I've missed you, Nolee."

"Me, too," she whispered, her voice hoarse. Clearly he hadn't forgotten exactly how to stir up a strong response from her, and her body remembered him, too, his touch just as she'd replayed it all these years.

Suddenly it didn't matter what had happened before or what would happen tomorrow. How much he understood about her or couldn't. What she wanted was to lose herself in the here and now, and to wring every ounce of pleasure from it that she could.

He lowered his face to kiss her full on the mouth while his fingers settled between her legs again. Sparks lit behind her eyes. He drew her tongue into his mouth and sucked gently, making her hips writhe in automatic response. She drenched his hand with her want.

He broke their kiss, skimmed his lips down her torso, then paused between her thighs. At the first flick of his tongue, the shudders started. She arched back, her hips re-flexively thrusting forward as he delved deeper. Probed longer. Pleasure tore through her in relentless waves, fed by his tongue administering long, sensual strokes. She couldn't tell where one delectable pulse of her senses stopped and the next one began. She only knew her body undulated with streams of pleasure.

Fingers fisted in his hair, knees slung over his shoul-ders, she shook as Dylan coaxed her to a fiery orgasm. Her pelvis contracted so hard she twisted atop her quilt, her fingers gripping for something to hold on to before she dropped into sweet, pulsating oblivion.

Finally, when her body was spent, she slumped, bone-less, against her pillows. The thick bedcovering bunched beneath her hips. Her legs sprawled helter-skelter across her mattress and her mind drifted, wasted by utter and total bliss.

She'd rediscovered a depth of pleasure she hadn't expe-rienced since Dylan left, yet still she craved more. Loop-ing her arms around his neck, she drew him down on top of her, coaxing his mouth to hers again.

"Take me," she whispered, no longer able to deny her-self or him any longer. Her senses were too overloaded, her thoughts too scrambled with memories, feelings—and deep, hungry need.

"With pleasure," he agreed, his husky voice full of naughty promise.

Vaguely, she sensed him undressing the rest of the way as she rained kisses over him, his heart thundering against hers as she tugged him closer, his naked upper body a taut block of sinewy muscle.

And then he was there between her thighs, his massive erection hot and hard. Every inch as thick and long as she remembered. A whimper escaped her throat, and she reached to touch him, feel him, stroke him into doing what she wanted. When he withdrew to roll on a condom, she nearly cried out with the aching loss her body felt.

An instant later, he loomed over her again, his sex sheathed and ready. Guiding her hips so that they angled toward him, he thrust inside her in one smooth motion. Her gasp grew into a shriek of delight at the way he stretched and filled her.

Suddenly she didn't know if she would laugh or cry at the sense of homecoming. Of understanding and silent knowing. Their bodies recognizing each other. Communicating. Hers opening up to him, more vulnerable than she ever allowed herself to be. How she'd missed him, she thought. Missed this.

Slowly he withdrew, his eyes locked with hers, then buried himself again, deeper still, the tip of his cock so deep it pressed against her cervix. Delirious with the hard satin feel of him and the lush sensations he inspired, Nolee clung to Dylan, trusting him to bring them to new heights with each strong thrust of his hips.

Her eyes closed as he slid into her again, the exquisite pleasure made all the stronger by his slow and measured withdrawal, a torturous, almost military precision that was new. And excruciating. And thrilling. She wriggled beneath him, ready to take charge and give him the same kind of soaring bliss he was giving her, but he held her fast to maintain control.

And heaven help her, she couldn't argue with someone who made her feel so…amazing. So ripe with lush sensuality. A woman, not a fisherman. Not a captain, or a lost girl who didn't belong to anyone. Oh, how she wanted to belong to Dylan. Still. He hadn't forgotten her. Them. Their old rhythms returned, the pleasure more acute, sharp, nearly painful for having gone so long without it.

He pinned her wrists over her head, stretching her out under his gaze and his touch while he brought his thrusts to a new level, picking up the tempo until her breath came in soft pants.

The air in the room changed, becoming electrically charged. The windowpane rattled with the wind and a cargo ship bellowed out from the distant sea. Nolee couldn't staunch the growing tightness in her core, the coiled pleasure just waiting to untwine with the slightest—

"Ooh!" She was free-falling into a sea of spasms again, her whole body reverberating with the forceful waves of pleasure.

Dylan stilled above her, his wide cock straining impossibly inside her before he, too, couldn't hold off his orgasm any longer. His whole gorgeous body shuddered with the strength of it, his hot chest coming to rest over hers.

Nolee's world tipped with the gradual recognition of what had happened between them. It was still there after all this time, that incredible emotional connection. She wouldn't have imagined it possible. The thought terrified her.

"Come here." Dylan's words rumbled thick and sexy in her ear, and he lowered himself beside her and pulled her into the tight circle of his arms. Enfolding her, sheltering her, his body curved around hers.

As if he could ever be a safe port for her heart, a place for her body to truly rest unguarded.

Only Dylan wielded such control over her and by sleeping with him tonight, she'd put herself at his mercy. She was an active participant in their worlds colliding again. And while she would make sure they proceeded with business as usual in the morning on the boat, Nolee knew nothing would ever be the same between them again.

"WELCOME TO THE DUTCH, son," Dylan said, clapping a heaving newbie, Tim Anders, on the back the following week. After seven days of grueling repair work, training crew and passing inspection, the *Pacific Dawn* had steamed out of port yesterday. They now drove through twenty-five-foot swells toward setting their first string of pots—about a hundred and fifteen miles northwest of Dutch Harbor.

Sniffing the briny air, feeling the chill, breeze-blown sea mist on his face, the slick deck rolling beneath his feet, Dylan relished the sheer size of the ocean. As a rescue swimmer, he was usually crouched inside a Jayhawk above it, his short bursts of intense water activity focused on rescuing others. But this—this enormous, ever-changing view—woke him up, his nerves jangling, stinging, as if he'd fallen asleep without knowing it.

He scanned the iridescent horizon, the dawning sky the color of a pearl, and swiped stinging salt water from his eyes. The sea was a sullen blue. Choppy and dull. The pitching deck kept the crew scrambling to keep their footing as heavy waves crashed over the rails, clawing and pounding at the vessel.

How was Nolee faring?

She'd been at the wheel for over eight hours and would go another eight before they finished today. He cast a quick glance up at the pilothouse window, glimpsing her outline through the spray-soaked glass as she steered the *Pacific*

Dawn on this all-important set. It was anyone's guess, at the start of the official season, where to locate a hot streak of crab. Experienced captains relied on old charts. Less experienced followed the fleet, listening in on radio channels to hear where other vessels hit it big.

Nolee, however, had gone in her own direction, miles from the rest of the fishing vessels, refusing his advice to radio his Uncle Bill for help.

No surprise there.

She seemed bent on doing things her own way, going it alone as she always had. It shouldn't have caught him off guard when he'd woken alone the morning after their sensual escapade. Gone was the passionate, uninhibited woman who'd taken him by storm. In her place stood a stone-faced Nolee, Captain Nolee, who barked orders at her crew. She'd refused to meet his gaze when she'd taken him aside and told him sex had been a mistake, one she wouldn't repeat or discuss again. Or any other topic. Including Craig.

Logic said to leave Nolee alone. They were friends. Or used to be. Definitely not lovers, despite that unforgettable night. Things between them hadn't changed. She'd still never leave Kodiak for him, and he wouldn't stay for her. But how to forget the most incredible sex of his life? The only woman to bring him such mind-blowing satisfaction?

He couldn't stop reliving it, his body wracked with desire, desperate and hungry for more, his need for her far from quenched.

No.

It'd only increased. Being out at sea, working side by side, made his need even more demanding, the urge to have her all-consuming. He had to focus, to complete his mission aboard the *Pacific Dawn*. Train and supervise staff. Haul crab. Leave Nolee and Kodiak without a backward glance when he transferred to the States, with no worry, concern or regrets.

Yeah. Right.

Deep down, he knew he still wanted answers about Craig. For closure, he assured himself.

Did dudes care about that shit?

This one did.

"Aim it at the bait grinder. Your puke's gotta have some herring in it," called Flint.

At the old fisherman's reference to the bait they'd made Tim bite the head off, a start-of-season tradition, the college dropout hurled another volley across the sea-washed deck. The boat rolled to the left and a wave smacked over the bow then retreated, carrying the mess with it.

"Bait!" hollered Tyler, one of the more experienced on deck. Which wasn't saying a lot. Unlike all but Flint and the relief captain, Stu, he'd at least been on a crab-fishing boat before. He and Jo, a long, lanky woman with a mop of black curly hair and serious eyes, guided the steel trap toward the launcher. It dangled from a blue crane operated by their engineer, Wesley.

"Coming up!" Dylan shouted and propelled a green-faced Tim to the ice chest, which held stacks of thirty-pound cod and fifty-pound frozen bait blocks used in their setups. "You're on," he shouted above the roaring engine.

Tim wiped his mouth with the sleeve of his slicker and stumbled away.

Dylan swerved back to the rails to oversee the important first launch. Green-and-yellow-raingear-clad crew gathered there, skidding feet encased in black rubber boots, hoods pulled up over ball caps, the men's faces shrouded in dripping beards. With only three weeks to fish and a large quota to make, they had to get this right.

"Keep an eye out," he barked when a swinging pot

nearly decapitated an approaching Tim. Headless carcasses dangled from each hand as he trudged across the angling deck. Like the other greenhorns, he struggled to find his footing as he tried going one way and the boat pushed him in the opposite direction. It'd be a miracle if he wasn't washed overboard on his first day.

Dylan swore under his breath. One newbie was dangerous enough, but a crew full of them? Suicide. A huge gamble. One he wouldn't let Nolee take alone. Crab fishing was one of the deadliest jobs in the world. A huge payoff coupled with greater risk. It tempted the inexperienced to give it a shot, but few could hang with the Bering Sea. How would their fledgling crew perform? This first day would tell the tale.

"Let's see what you're made of!" bawled Flint.

"Off the rails!" came Nolee's order over the PA and they scrambled backward as a tall wave pelted them. Tyler grabbed the crane and pulled his feet up and out of the way. Jo and Flint looped their arms through tethered cages. Tim nearly toppled and Dylan steadied the kid as the arctic water doused them.

"That was a curler," boomed Stu, hooting with the rest of the group as the dragging water receded. He was bearded and paunchy, a short, stout man with humorous eyes.

Tim shoved himself backward inside the loaded pot, hooked the two cod in the center and scuttled out.

"After a hundred pots today, that won't be a bad workout," drawled Flint, a limp cigarette clamped between his pale lips.

"Okay guys," came Nolee's voice over the PA system. "First pot of this opi season. Let her go!"

The crew whooped while Jo and Tyler secured the trapdoor. An impromptu dance broke out, Flint leading the way as he pinched his fingers together overhead and shuffled left then right.

"Do the crabby dance, Tim!" yelled a red-faced Tyler as he did some kind of jig that made even stoic Jo smile.

"For good luck!" Flint snapped a hand beneath the boy's nose.

"Nah," Tim said, shaking his head, his face leached of color.

The *Pacific Dawn* tilted again, and the boat groaned as another swell rose and smacked them straight across the chins.

"You just got sea-kissed," guffawed Flint as Tim blinked blindly through the water streaming off his brow.

"We're naming this set 'Tim's puke string' for good luck," added Stu. He tugged the last knot on the pot door tight, then turned. "Let's see if it gets us a little somethin' somethin'."

Stu signaled to Wesley, who now manned the hydraulics, and the launcher tilted toward the ocean with a mechanical whine. The steel trap toppled, splatted into the choppy ocean, then disappeared below the agitated murk.

Dylan snatched the attached red buoy and white marker and hurled them after the disappearing pot.

Bring us some crab, he thought, sending that silent wish down to the depths with it.

"Rig the pots. Next launch in three minutes," Dylan ordered as Nolee steamed ahead.

"If that wheel ain't turnin' then we ain't earnin'," added Stu with a wink.

"Gotta fill the tank to put money in the bank," Flint mumbled as he cupped his hand around his mouth and tried relighting his cigarette for the third time, the brisk wind snatching the flame away.

"Let's go, boys!" Dylan called, "and gal," and the group raced to launch the next pot.

Eight hours later, Dylan poured himself a cup of coffee in the cramped galley and turned, nearly bumping into a freshly showered Nolee. Any lethargy he'd felt earlier vanished at the sight of her. Dark tendrils of hair clung to her dusky cheeks. Wet spiky lashes framed her beautiful brown eyes. The scent of her shampoo rose from her damp head and he shoved his hands into his pockets, willing himself not to reach for her.

The rich, creamy smell of Flint's clam chowder filled the small space, dominated by overflowing cabinets and a small, built-in seating area that held five of the seven crew members. They clutched the table, which was clamped to the floor, arms shooting out to stop salt, pepper or mugs sliding off. The floor hummed with an almost constant vibration, the engine noise juddering below their feet.

Nolee's eyes, when they met Dylan's, were raw and red-rimmed from exhaustion. The temptation to haul her upstairs to her quarters and wipe away her fatigue in the most pleasurable way possible seized him. He wanted to still her nervous hands and shifting feet with a kiss that would render her senseless. He settled for grabbing her a cup of coffee, wondering what had gotten into him that he was pursuing a woman who was exactly all wrong for him.

"Thank you," she said, her husky voice rough with strain. She'd worked eighteen hours straight, but no one would know it from her rigid back and set chin unless they looked closely, the way he was.

"You're welcome." He sank his eyes into hers.

Their fingertips grazed, a light touch that reminded him he hadn't gotten to do half the things he wanted to do with her the other night. When he closed his eyes, he saw her flushed, passionate face. The arch of her neck when he'd buried himself inside her. Her throaty cries in his ear. The sweet smell of her breath as she'd fallen asleep in his arms like she belonged there.

She sidled by, grabbed a bowl and ladled herself some chowder. After snagging a spoon from the drawer, she turned and leaned against the cabinets, her gaze sweeping over the hunched crew.

"Good job, boys." And then, with a tired smile, she added, "Better get some shut-eye. We'll be hauling 'em back out in six."

Flint's dark frown snuffed out the greenhorns' groans. "Nice work yourself, Captain."

She crumbled oyster crackers into her soup. "How are you feeling, Tim?"

Dylan watched the crew member closely. Tim struggled to sit straighter, gave up and winced, holding the ribs Dylan had taped a couple of hours ago after two fifty-pound blocks of frozen cod fell on him in the freezer. "Okay, I guess."

No wheezing or difficulty breathing. Not a punctured lung. It could have been far, far worse.

"Hydro, magic," guffawed Tyler and the rest of the table burst out laughing at the reference to the painkiller. "We'll have you hooking and sorting tomorrow."

"We'll see," mused Nolee, her expression thoughtful. "If he's not better, you'll be working a five-man deck."

The boat's back-and-forth motion sent a bottle of hot sauce spinning off the table.

"Agreed. I'll reevaluate before the shift," Dylan interjected, snatching the jar before it hit the laminate floor. As a level-one EMT, he could spot a major complication, like pneumothorax, before it put the crew member in jeopardy.

"We'll handle it," Stu put in as he clomped inside the wheelhouse to take the next shift at the wheel for Nolee.

He shed his oilskin, bringing with him the cold, damp air, his face shining with sea spray.

Dylan's eyes met Nolee's and then her lashes dropped, her gaze sliding away. She leaned an arm on a stack of plates as the boat rocked. He didn't have to read her mind to know what she thought. What they both thought.

A six-man crew full of rookies was hard enough. Down an extra man and their already difficult task became near to impossible. Yet he'd push on as he knew Nolee would. They were in it together, he silently communicated to her bent head.

Dylan rose as Nolee headed outside. He donned a coat, shoved down the latch and emerged onto the unlit deck.

The bitter fresh air assailed him, and he could feel the briny scent float into his nose. Tasted the salt on his lips. Heard the ceaseless waves churning the vast black sea.

At last he spied Nolee leaning against the far end of the pilothouse. Her hair had fallen across her face, half concealing a worried frown as she stared out at the seagulls swooping alongside the ship. She glanced up at him sharply when he joined her.

He raised his voice above the thumping and grinding engines and said, "Great job today."

She shook her head before releasing a long breath. "Do you think we'll need to take Tim back to port for an X-ray?"

He thought of the tens of thousands of dollars she stood to lose if they had to head back now. "Can't say yet. But it's possible," he said, then added, "There are real consequences to consider, for other people beyond yourself, when taking big risks…" He wondered if perhaps he also meant himself.

When she looked at him, the full force of her concern hit him square on. "You think I don't care about the crew?"

Do you care about me? he nearly asked, but clamped his lips shut. He tried hard to keep his breath steady in his chest. "You said I didn't know you. Let me know you again."

Above them, in the Alaskan sky, the stars glittered like ballroom lights, bathing the seas with silver. Unable to keep his distance any longer, he pushed back her hood and slid a hand down her cheek before he hauled her up against him. The feel of her pressed to him didn't compare with the sexy gasp from her lips. The sound tripped down his spine like a lover's fingertip.

"Why didn't you tell me about Craig?"

Her lids lifted. Eyes flared and she stiffened. Pulled back. "It's not my fault if you make snap decisions about people…rushing to judgment and turning your back on them."

Stunned, he stared at her. So their split was now his fault?

Tense silence crackled between them, broken only by the sound of the sea and the boat cutting a white swath through the ocean. A strangled noise escaped her and with an anguished look, she shoved him away and escaped back inside.

He stared into the black night. Breathed out, bracing himself against the movement of the ship. Turned into the arctic wind blasting from the north.

Had he broken Nolee's heart? All these years he'd thought himself the wounded party. Betrayed. How would his life be different if he'd taken the time to understand instead of running from the first sign of rejection from someone he loved?

And would he want his life to be different? The thumping and banging of his heart answered.

He stared out at the diamond-freckled sky, the white foam trailing through inky waters.

He hadn't thought he had regrets.

But now he wondered.

If she hadn't made the choice for him, would he have been happy staying with her in Kodiak?

Doubt slipped in like an eel. He shoved it back. His feelings were irrelevant. His life was set.

Nolee hadn't wanted him. Still didn't, given her about-face after they'd made love.

No matter how much a part of him might wish otherwise.

9

"WE'VE GOT A hundred pots to pull and good weather to do it," Nolee instructed the bleary-eyed crew the next morning. "But don't let the calm fool you. It's still deadly out there. Be careful on the rail and keep your footing."

Twenty-four hours had passed since she'd set her first string. Time to bring the traps aboard and see if her gamble to fish in this distant spot paid off. Nerves rippled in her stomach. Concentric, nauseating rings.

Please, please, give us a big haul.

Dylan leaned against the galley's small double sink. There was a current of sexual tension that caused their eyes to keep meeting and sliding away, then meeting again. Nolee's skin flushed warm and she felt a heightened awareness of everything: the smells of coffee and bacon, the edge of his thermal shirt against the bronzed skin of his neck, her own hand reaching for the sugar.

With his fitted, long-sleeved shirt accentuating ridges and rises in all the right places, dark scruff on his lean jaw, his cropped curls tousled, Dylan had that just-rolled-out-of-bed, rumpled, sexy-as-hell look. Her heartbeat pounded loudly in her ears, the memory of that hard male body pressed up against her still tormenting her every waking minute.

For a moment she let herself fantasize about staying inside today. Locking herself in her private quarters with the powerful, compelling swimmer. Having him all to herself. The room was 90 percent bed and what she wanted to do to him on it… A bolt of desire hit her right between the thighs. Looking into his heated eyes, she imagined he was thinking the same thing, and it was all she could do to keep herself from flushing scarlet.

Keep your head in the game.

Eye on the prize.

Dylan was a momentary fling, she told herself. Something she could fantasize about but never have again. She had to focus on her job, her life, and especially her heart, which could all too easily fall for Dylan again if she wasn't careful.

"Let's do it!" Flint shouted, fired up. He smacked rough weathered hands together in a loud clap.

"What about Tim?" asked Jo as she emerged, dressed, from the shower, rubbing her long wet hair with a towel. Wesley dropped his bacon slice and stared at her, mouth open, until Tyler nudged him and guffawed.

Dylan finished his oatmeal and turned to the sink. "He's staying in the rack today," he said over his shoulder.

"I believe he's feeling a bit better," Wesley put in, looking a bit recovered, the tips of his ears a bright pink. His eyes hadn't left Jo.

"A bruised rib. Possibly a hairline fracture. Another day of rest and he'll be good to go," Dylan said, his commanding baritone filling the room as easily as his brawny body.

Nolee had been so relieved when Dylan gave her Tim's update a half hour ago, her knees had turned to jelly. He was stable, but she'd erred on the side of caution and given him the day to recuperate, even though it'd slow her down and cost more time…

And money.

Would the reduced crew be able to pull off this demanding day?

Flint and Wesley swapped an uneasy look. Resolve fired through her. Hesitation, fear, second-guessing—they had no place in crab fishing. Not with the margin of error, the price of your livelihood, your life, razor thin. It was time to talk tough.

"Stay on board and just run," she directed, squaring her jaw and raising her chin. Her gaze swept over the crew, keeping eye contact until they each nodded at her. Sat up straighter. "That's all you have to do. Good luck. Stay safe."

Dylan stowed his dish and turned to the crew. "Green light!" he barked. The galvanized group scrambled. They grabbed their raingear from hooks by the portal and bolted outside.

He was good with the crew, she mused. After yesterday's grueling slog, the newbies could have woken sullen, in pain and unmotivated. Yet they'd responded well to her and Dylan. No matter the tensions and secrets between them, they still made a damn good team. Could she have done this without him?

No, came the swift, unsettling answer. She swatted it away. She wouldn't be dependent on Dylan. Or anyone.

"Just remember. Fishing isn't life-or-death…" He drew close, placed a calloused finger under her chin and tipped it up so that she met his warm eyes. Awareness skittered down her spine to pool at its base and tingle through her hips.

"…it's more important," she finished for him, breathless. She couldn't stop her mouth from quirking at the corny saying Captain Bill used when they'd fished with him on the *Easy Rider*.

They'd thought it crazy then, but now, in light of everything…it didn't sound so nuts.

Dylan's eyes lingered on her lips, then rose. The slow drag of his gaze set her alight. He stroked a fingertip up the side of her neck and watched her as she shivered in response to the feathery caress. The musky scent of his soap tempted her, making her knees weak with the urge to wrap herself around him.

Right here. Right now.

The rest of the world be damned.

Her smile faded and Dylan gathered her hands in his. He brushed his thumb over her knuckles, and she nearly died at the sexy promise in his eyes. The heat they'd ignited last week simmered again, reminding her it wasn't going away anytime soon.

"Kick ass, Nolee," he said, his voice tender. Gruff. Deep.

Blinking, she tried to ignore the hedonistic wants of her body to make sense of his words.

"Same, asshole," she murmured shakily, another of their old exchanges from easier times…when life and love hadn't become so damn complicated.

His eyes gleamed and then, with a wink, he squeezed her hands, turned and followed the fishermen out the door. She stared at the closed portal and shivered at the blast of cold, damp air that'd curled inside before he shut the door.

Move it, girl.

She gave herself a little shake, grabbed another cup of coffee and headed upstairs. A moment later, she dropped into her captain's chair, blew on her steaming coffee and set it beside her radar screen. Around her, the dials and maps of the pilothouse stared back mutely, oblivious of the day's significance. A clockwise sweeping band updated the monitor.

Nolee peered through her salt-crusted pilot window at the calm blue sea, her belly anything but settled. Last night, she'd tossed and turned, her tumbling thoughts making her dizzy and a little sick as she'd replayed her conversation with Dylan. How much longer could she avoid telling him the truth about their breakup?

She'd seduced him rather than discuss her real reasons for not setting him straight about Craig. But it'd gone too far. Their night of decadent pleasure now left her aching for him, craving more. Yet she couldn't be that emotionally vulnerable with him. Wouldn't go down that painful road again.

The more he questioned, the more she questioned herself.

Dylan's tall, sleek frame appeared below. The sun came out from behind a cloud and she had to squint to see him properly. The tight knit cap he'd donned accentuated his gorgeous angular face. His hearty laugh boomed through her speaker. Long strides carried him effortlessly across the sea-washed deck as he pointed this way and that to the scuttling crew. They hurried to obey his every order.

God, she wanted him. That hadn't changed. Nor had her regrets.

Had she been wrong to let him think she'd been cheating with Craig? She'd been furious at his quick assumption back then, but she couldn't level all the blame on Dylan.

Deep down, she'd feared he might tempt her to leave. Her mother's observation that Nolee had other reasons for refusing to move away returned to her. Could some of that be fear of the unknown? A dread for moving from house to house as she had growing up, never one space, one home, to call her own?

She shoved open a porthole. Time to clear her head. Focus.

Crisp sea air wafted inside the wheelhouse. Seagulls shrieked and dive-bombed the low-breaking crests. She blinked stinging eyes and studied the bustling crew. Behind them, the skies were clearing to a bright, vivid blue, the sea becalmed. It was the kind of sight that filled the heart with optimism. Yet Nolee couldn't feel settled with so much in question.

And right now, besides her resurging feelings for Dylan, the biggest question mark was today's catch.

She read the GPS coordinates she'd noted in her logbook yesterday and scanned her monitor. Closing in. They'd arrive at the start of the string in a couple of minutes.

She pulled down her gooseneck mic. "Ready crew. Coming up on our first pot."

Dylan turned and gave her a thumbs-up, his killer smile flashing beneath the heartbreaking blue of the sky. "Roger, Captain."

Her breath caught at the sun dancing on his handsome face, the sparkle in his eyes. He was in his element here. Rugged. Untamed. Proud. He might not think of himself as a product of Alaska, but he was. Every gorgeous inch of him.

Wesley scrambled to the winch while Tyler lit a cigarette with a welding torch before passing it to Flint. Jo paused to speak to Wesley a moment, the two briefly touching hands before she headed to the rail.

Nolee's adrenaline surged. The first red-and-white marker appeared off her starboard side. She slowed her engine speed and maneuvered over the pot. Their first haul had the potential to set the emotional tone for the crew for the entire trip. Full, and they'd be hyped up and excited; empty, and they'd be anxious and discouraged.

Come on. Come on...

Dylan grabbed a grapple hook and she guided the *Pa-*

cific Dawn closer, working with the current, the wind. Forty feet out. Thirty. Twisting at the waist, he let loose, hurling it toward the drifting line.

"Hooked it!" shouted Flint and she grinned, euphoria glowing so bright inside it made her blink fast. Dylan had always been the best thrower she knew; he hadn't let her down.

She waited, breathless, as he reeled it in, hand over hand, until he had enough line to pass to Flint.

The older sailor threaded the dripping rope into the winch's spinning gears and the unmistakable click, click, click rattled through her PA system. She eyed the ship's edge and waited for a glimpse of this all-important first pot.

Let it be filled...

More grinding. It sounded heavy.

"Let's see what we got, boys!" she hollered into the PA.

"Come on, Krabby Patty!" shouted Tyler, jumping up and down from both excitement and cold, Nolee guessed.

Her heart drummed.

The top of the cage appeared and her breath seized.

"Here we go!" Jo called.

"Survey says..." Flint thundered.

She stared intently as the pot rose over the starboard side, dripping, seaweed dangling from it, half full.

Half full!

"YeeeeeeAAH!" roared the group.

"That's what's up!"

"Yes, it is."

The exalting crew began shoveling the waving, squirming gray crab out of the pot and onto the sorting table. All but Dylan cheered.

"All I'm seeing is dollar bills!"

"First pot of the opi season—how 'bout that!"

She labored to keep the boat in position, waiting to see if the haul was good enough for them to set the pot back in the same spot. Cautious excitement built, but she kept it in check. She closely watched the inexperienced crew. A large haul and a good haul weren't always the same thing.

The sorting table would tell the tale.

The cheers faded as they hooked the metal table to the tank chute.

"What's it look like?" she asked anxiously.

Dylan shook his head, disappointment weighing down his sculpted features. He cupped his hands around his mouth and yelled, "Mostly juvenile males. Some females."

The reality walloped her like a punch, and she swore through gritted teeth. The worst possible catch. If they hadn't found a school of legals, then a thankless day stretched ahead full of backbreaking work, unloading crab they couldn't keep.

"Tim!" Flint hollered. "Your puke string sucks!"

Within minutes they'd sorted the catch. Illegals, undersized males or any size females were tossed into the wastebin and dumped overboard. The rest were flung into the tank.

"How many?" she asked wearily.

Dylan held up three fingers, then made a circle with his hand.

"Thirty?" she repeated dully, just to be sure of the dismal number. Her stomach base jumped and splatted somewhere near her feet. She needed to average two hundred a pot to meet her quota.

Dylan nodded slowly and she averted her gaze. Noted the number in her logbook. She didn't have to see his face to know the expression he wore. It must mirror her own feelings. Concern. Disappointment…and maybe…justifiably for him…a bit of an I-told-you-so.

"Don't set it back." She scribbled the dismal number in her logbook then drove the boat to the next marker as Dylan turned back to the crew.

He'd advised her to ask for help in locating the schools. She hadn't wanted anyone else's advice or guidance, though.

Why? came the swift question.

Her old childhood feeling of helplessness, powerlessness arose. A dark specter.

She'd always considered independence an asset. Relying on people put you at their mercy, your life theirs to control. Yet now she wondered if her determination to go it alone could also be a liability. Did she actually need others like Captain Bill? Dylan even?

And was it safe?

She liked having Dylan on board. He was a natural. Clearly, he belonged here and she wished he belonged to her, too... But he'd be gone soon, his dislike of Kodiak as bone-deep as her love of this place. Given his transfer plans, and her resolve to stay, they could never work. She wouldn't waste time trying to change his mind.

No matter how sorely Dylan Holt tempted her.

"COME ON, BUD. One more bottle. Drink until it hurts."

Dylan sat up in his bunk at the sound of Nolee's voice coming through the wall a few days later. The ship swayed, the engines burbled and his roommates slept on heavily. He peered at the battery-operated alarm clock. Hours left until dawn. No one should be awake except for the relief captain, Stu, who helmed the boat now. Especially Nolee. She'd just finished another fifteen-hour shift driving them back to fishing grounds after meeting their first offload date in Dutch Harbor.

And it'd been a dismal, disappointing one at that. Their

low count and meager payout from the seafood processing plant had kept her on the phone most of the afternoon, re-assuring her bosses. When he tried taking her aside, she'd dodged the attempt as she had the past few days.

So who was she talking to now?

He slid out of his bunk and padded silently into the pitch-dark galley. Light spilled from the berth beside his. Stu's bunk was empty. Jo snored softly on a top bunk. Tyler twisted atop his bed frame, holding his calf, face contorted.

Leg cramps.

Dehydration.

Dylan swore beneath his breath. He should have no-ticed signs. They'd all been preoccupied as they'd hustled to ready pots ahead of another grinding day tomorrow. Though that was no excuse for anyone getting sick on his watch.

The fact that a heavy-lidded Nolee, who'd chatted and cracked jokes with the crew at dinner despite her evident exhaustion, had spotted the problem, caught him off guard. Kept his bare feet rooted to the floor as he stood silent wit-ness to this unexpected exchange.

She was dressed, as always, in her sexy tough-guy gear that did nothing to conceal her shape. Her body was the kind men went stupid over. Lush high breasts filled out a black tank top that accentuated her muscular arms. Low-riding camouflage pants cupped the sweet curve of her ass and revealed a mouthwatering glimpse of toned stomach. The top of her anchor tattoo peeked above the waistband. Her long black hair was all over the place, a tangled mass that tumbled past her shoulders.

She shoved a jar of green liquid into Tyler's hand.

A rueful grin spread across Dylan's face. Pickle juice. A fisherman's remedy for muscle cramps.

"Come on," she urged. "Down the hatch."

Tyler lurched upright, grabbed the drink and sipped. When he tried handing it back to Nolee, she shook her head, her mouth set in that firm way he recognized all too well. She was a tough cookie. But she had her tender side, too.

And an intoxicating, wanton nature that exhilarated him. Kept him on a high state of alert. And ready.

Semper Paratus.

His groin tightened.

He was always ready for her.

"All of it," Nolee urged, tipping her beautiful face. The artificial light gleamed on her cheekbones. Cast shadows beneath her dark, magnetic eyes.

Tyler finished it off then flopped back on his pillow. The jar tumbled from his fingers. Green liquid trickled onto his brown coverlet. He shoved his hands behind his head and screwed his eyes shut.

"Better?"

Tyler's nod swerved into a head shake. "I want to quit."

Nolee froze, halfway to standing, then perched back on the bunk. Dylan's heart thudded. They couldn't lose more crew. Tim still worked at limited capacity with his rib injury. And who the hell knew when another newbie might get hurt or worse? Even an experienced hand like himself?

Shit happened.

Dylan waited for a classic Nolee ass chewing, already feeling sorry for the greenhorn. What she said next, however, made his mouth drop.

"Me, too, sometimes."

Tyler's eyes cracked open. "No way."

"You calling me a liar?"

"Nah. It's just. You're Captain Arnauyq."

"And you're Tyler Sanders. A Bering Sea badass. One of us now, dude."

His lids rose further and a snort-laugh escaped him. "An ass maybe. I couldn't hook more than a couple of pots all week. Dylan had to do almost all of 'em."

Reflexively, Dylan rubbed his sore biceps and nearly strode in to assure Tyler. He was doing great for his level of experience and fitness. He shouldn't compare himself to Dylan.

As a Coast Guard swimmer, he was trained for numbing endurance work. He needed it, in fact. It was why he worked out four to six hours a day until his body became a highly efficient instrument, designed for arduous life-and-death rescues. A civilian and a rescuer weren't in the same league. But Tyler's mental toughness was half the battle. He needed to know that.

But out of respect for Nolee, Dylan waited to see what she said next.

She shrugged. "So you'll get it tomorrow. Or the next day. You think anyone gets anything perfectly on the first try?"

"Some do."

She blew a dangling strand of hair out of her face and crossed her arms over her chest. "Well. We hate those people."

Tyler laughed and Dylan bit back his own chuckle. Yes. He and Nolee had bonded over their mutual dislike of people who had it easy.

When he'd opened up about his favored brother, confided about his hypercritical oppressive father, the man who'd called Dylan a waste of space, she'd listened.

Commiserated.

Urged him to stop living in others' shadows and pursue his own path. Even if it carried him away from her.

She lifted her chin and eyed Tyler down her strong nose. "You've got what it takes."

His heart twisted at her encouragement. She'd had faith in him like that when no one, except his uncle, had… And how had he repaid that support? With distrust. Withdrawal. Blame without even once stopping to ask for her side of the story.

He'd always assumed life would dish him out the worst. It might be an ideal mindset for a high-stakes rescuer who needed to anticipate every scenario. But it'd let him down when it came to Nolee. No. *He'd* let himself down. Then and now.

He'd jumped to conclusions.

Hadn't asked the right questions. Hadn't asked *any* questions.

He'd stopped persisting with them now, too.

But that ended tonight. He would seek Nolee out and get to the bottom of it. More important than getting answers, though, was what *he* needed to give *her*.

An apology.

"You think so?" Tyler rubbed his eyes hard.

"No one else had the guts to sign on with me after the ship went down."

"Except Flint and Stu."

"Stu's a stubborn cuss and Flint's just plain crazy."

Tyler's laugh was huge. Walloping. Nolee joined him, the sexy sound of her merriment teasing awake Dylan's senses. Heat rushed over his skin.

He'd forgotten how funny she could be. Caring, despite the fierce independence that hid her softer side.

And so damn hot.

Suddenly Tyler sat up and lifted his calf. Turned it. "Hey. My leg doesn't hurt."

Nolee's eyes lit from within and her mouth curved. "Good, because I'm putting you on the grapple hook again this week."

Tyler ducked his head. "Can I ask you something else?"

"Sure."

His eyes rolled up to meet hers. "You think maybe I got what it takes to—uh—be a captain someday?"

Nolee angled her head and studied him a minute, as if taking his measure. Tyler's clenched hands bunched the blanket fabric. He seemed not to breathe. Neither did Dylan.

At last she nodded. "Someone once told me something I've never forgotten."

Tyler's eyes widened and he nodded for her to continue.

"Never, *never*, NEVER give up."

Nolee.

Those words.

Brow scrunched, Tyler eyed her. Skeptical. "Uh. Okay."

"Winston Churchill said that."

And me, Dylan thought. He'd quoted that to Nolee when they'd battled through a particularly rough run their first year together as greenhorns. She'd been ready to quit, and he'd just realized how much he'd needed her to stay.

She hadn't forgotten.

And nor should he.

He'd given up. Quit on her. Remorse swamped him but surging feelings pushed it back. He didn't have a lot of time left in Kodiak, but he wouldn't waste another moment of it without Nolee.

"'Night, Captain."

She stood and Dylan slunk back in the shadows, not wanting to be caught eavesdropping on Tyler's personal moment. It would humiliate the guy.

He held his breath as Nolee swerved to the wheelhouse entrance and jogged up the stairs without seeing him.

He shifted his weight from one foot to another. His

thoughts chugged as hard as the gears thrumming beneath the floorboards.

Tyler's lights flicked off and Dylan crept up the passage after Nolee. His blood pounded through his veins with a near-audible swish.

He was done waiting.

Time for answers.

And no distractions.

In fact, if anyone did the distracting…this time, it'd be him.

10

NOLEE KICKED OFF her work boots and camo pants, flopped back on her captain's bunk and scooched up until her head sank into her thick pillow. The small, triangle-shaped stateroom bobbed gently with the motion of the sea. Lulling her. She breathed in the briny, woody smell of the slanted walls and a long exhale fluttered her lips as she stared up at the stars visible through her skylight.

What a long, arduous, thankless week.

It'd been humiliating and damn discouraging to offload such a meager haul yesterday. Word of their arrival in Dutch Harbor spread the moment they'd tossed their first line. Her bosses' phone call shouldn't have surprised her. For a moment, she'd contemplated sending them straight to voice mail. Avoid the lecture completely, just as she'd steered clear of a stern-faced Dylan. She didn't need their dire warnings, threats and reminders to fill the quota, or else.

And she especially wanted to avoid overly cautious Dylan's I-told-you-so. He'd never understand why she needed to take these risks and prove that she could do this on her own.

With her first opilio run a total bust, she had to hit a proverbial jackpot on this next string.

Where were those crab?

She opened the porthole beside her built-in bed and breathed the chilly, fresh air. Her stiff body relaxed. The ship dipped and rose gently in the sea. Engines drummed steadily underneath her berth, vibrating through her, chugging and groaning with effort.

At a knock on her door, she froze. The ship seemed to be running smoothly. She'd already dealt with her crew crisis. So now what?

She scrambled to her feet. "Who is it?" she called through the door.

"Dylan."

Her heart hammered as if clamoring to be heard. "Oh. I'm—uh—sleeping."

A pause. Then a low chuckle drifted through the panel. It moved through her body, melting her insides. "So that makes me a dream?"

The corners of her mouth lifted. Oh, yes. A very naughty one if it were true… She'd had quite a few lately that'd begun exactly like this, starring PO1 Dylan Holt.

"What's up?" she squeaked, then cleared her throat. Tried again. "What can I do for you?" There. Less pirate wench. More captain of the Bering Sea.

"We need to talk."

She looked around her small stateroom. The V-shaped bed dominated the space that held only crammed shelves and a narrow bureau. A small door led to her private bathroom and shower. Much, much too intimate.

"Isn't that something only women say?" she tried to joke, her voice catching, running out of air.

"I'm in touch with my feminine side," he protested in a very deep, very manly growl.

She laughed. "Yeah. Right. Listen. How about in the morning? We can—"

"I want to say I'm sorry, Nolee."

Whoa. Not what she expected at all. Faintness stole over her, and suddenly she couldn't feel her feet.

She yanked open the door before she could weigh the action. Dylan leaned against the jamb, filling the doorframe. His evergreen eyes burned dark in the dim light.

Her throat swelled. Desire pulsed between her thighs as his gaze dropped to her feet then slid upward. The slow, sexy perusal made her acutely aware that she wore only a wash-shrunken tank top and boy shorts. Her toes curled. The front of her shirt peaked over her beading nipples.

And the sight of him.

He was magnificent.

His bronze shoulders and defined abs, the ridges visible through the tight, thin material of his white tank, could have leaped off an action film screen. Or a televised MMA fight. No wonder he had won medals, saved countless lives. With a physique like that, he looked invincible. Powerful. A force unto himself.

Her body buzzed with hunger.

She needed to shut the door on him.

Fast.

He leaned close and shook her determination to smithereens.

"What did you say?" she found herself asking, her fuzzy head struggling to make sense of his words with her senses overwhelmed and bombarded.

Where were his recriminations? His I-told-you-so's?

And what was he apologizing for?

Dylan angled his head. "I'd rather speak in private."

She followed his over-the-shoulder glance and spotted the back of Stu's head above the captain's chair twenty feet away. He wore large headphones and nodded along to whatever music was streaming through them, his glance fixed on the wheelhouse's controls. Since the stairs from the galley opened behind him, he probably hadn't spied Dylan.

Yet.

But that could change in an instant. Nerves strung tight with anticipation, Nolee dragged Dylan inside and he followed, too close. Too large. Heat radiated off his powerful body. She needed to establish who was in charge here. This was her ship. Her space. Her body and heart. Not his.

She reached around him to pull the latch shut and came into contact with hard male chest.

"Where should I sit?" That husky rumble in her ear made her think about kissing him…in a thousand places besides his lips.

The angled walls seemed to close around them. She cleared her throat and breathed in a steadying gulp of air. Too bad his scent filtered through, seducing her senses.

Clean. Like soap rather than cologne. And sea-salty. His warm skin had tasted like the ocean. The Alaskan outdoors. A wild thrill skipped through her.

She was trapped in the smallest space imaginable with the sexiest man alive. Being with Dylan Holt in this berth was a fantasy come true, she had to admit. Despite every last one of her reservations, her body responded to his proximity.

"Take a seat." She nodded to her bed.

Dylan sank to the edge and leaned back to rest his weight on his elbows, endless legs sprawled in front of him, looking dangerous and sexy as hell. His white muscle tank rode up over a mouthwatering slab of abs that made her fingers itch to trace every dip and ridge of his stomach, follow that soft trail of hair that disappeared below the waistband of his pants.

She stood very still, as if somehow she could turn herself to stone and not feel every sizzling cell in her overheated body.

Dylan beckoned. "Join me?"

To mask her inner struggle, she backed away and created a breath of distance between them. "I'm fine."

After a brief moment of silence, he said, "I'm sorry about what happened with the whole Craig misunderstanding."

Confusion pulled her eyebrows together. She stared down at him. Puzzled. "You didn't cause it."

"Didn't I?"

She opened her mouth but gulped back her words as he shook his head.

"I shouldn't have jumped to conclusions," he continued, his guarded expression giving way to heartbreaking vulnerability. "Blamed you. You were my best friend. My first love. I let my hang-ups get in the way."

She melted at his words. He'd been her first love, too.

Turning, she sank down to the edge of the mattress beside him. Goose bumps rose across her skin at the feel of his firm arms brushing against hers.

"Which hang-ups?" She tried joking to ease the building tension. "Making hasty judgments? Always assuming the worst? Vanishing when someone hurts you?" She peered at him from beneath a raised brow and shrugged. "You have a bunch."

He rolled his eyes at her. "I'll take that." A growing arctic wind tossed the sea, spraying the porthole window and making Nolee shiver. She reached over Dylan to close it, then tipped sideways when the ship jogged. Desire kicked through her as his hands settled briefly on her waist, steadying her.

When she repositioned herself, he twisted around to face her. "I lumped you in with my family. Thought I wasn't good enough for you, either. I could never understand what you saw in me." She watched, mesmerized, as he slid his fingers into her hair and sank his eyes into hers. Immobility weighed her limbs, holding her in place.

"Everything. I saw everything in you, Dylan," she breathed, then melted against his chest.

His deliciously near-naked chest.

She knew she shouldn't be responding to those sexy pecs, or other appealing parts of Dylan. But as her heart jumped in her chest with their nearness, Nolee relished the adrenaline rush of their encounter. His muscular arms closed carefully around her. His heart thudded beneath her ear.

"I left without saying goodbye and put distance between me and the person I thought had hurt me. I made a snap judgment. It was wrong."

Sexual tension hummed between their bodies. Vibrated.

"So was I."

He tipped her head up so that their eyes met. He stared at her for several seconds before placing his bristled cheek next to her smooth one, so close that his lips caressed her ear as he spoke. His breath, warm and moist, rushed over her sensitive skin. "Why didn't you tell me the truth?"

"I didn't want you to miss the chance to get what you'd always wanted."

If he'd stayed, he would have been miserable and left her just the same, eventually. She hadn't wanted to be like her mother, abandoned and heartbroken. Yet, looking back, she'd ended up that way, regardless.

He pulled back, averted his head and briefly closed his

eyes. He looked like he might be sick. "What I wanted most was you," he rasped, his voice full of gravel, painful sharp stones.

They stared at each other wordlessly for a charged, tortured minute. Her heart leaked—no, hemorrhaged—in her chest. She blinked away the stinging rush in her eyes. He didn't mean that. Couldn't...

"Not the Coast Guard?"

He blew out a long breath, closed his eyes and shook his head. "No. I don't know. I guess we never will. Can't turn back time."

With a feeling in her stomach as if someone had tied a rock to it and thrown it overboard, she raced ahead, giving voice to her tumbling thoughts. "We each got the future we wanted. I'm captain of my own ship. You're traveling the world saving lives. Not stuck in Kodiak."

His thumb traced a slow trail over her cheek. Those glittering emerald eyes searched hers. They made her feel warm and liquid-filled, as though all her tension had been a solid thing and now was not.

"We're older now," she whispered.

"Wiser," he agreed. One eyebrow rose. His hands settled on the outside of her knees and skimmed their way up her thighs, pausing on her hips.

Her chest expanded on a deep inhalation of breath. She held it for a second before finally letting it all go in a slow, smooth stream of air. "We won't make the same mistakes we made before."

His fingers tightened on her hips. "No. We won't."

"We can do things differently." Her senses swam.

"So you're saying..."

The force of her need for him shook the fingers she slid up his biceps. What would it feel like to have this officer obey her every wicked whim? If she was in charge, surely she wouldn't be as vulnerable, in danger of giving him everything, including her heart.

"I can't fight this, Dylan." The fire he'd ignited inside her three weeks ago, the one that continued to smolder, could no longer be contained. The sensual flames licking over her flesh confirmed her assessment. "If we keep things physical-only, we can indulge a little while you're here." Her eyes dipped to his hard, handsome mouth. "We shouldn't waste the time we have left together."

"I like the sound of that." In one effortless move, he scooped her up and settled her in his lap. As she tilted her gaze up to his, she found him already staring down at her, his eyes searing into hers in the low light the full moon cast inside the room.

A small sound, something like a whimpering gasp, escaped her. He cupped a hand around the back of her head and drew her mouth to his before she could catch her breath. His tongue stroked over hers with slow, possessive thoroughness. What little air she had left in her lungs, he stole with his kiss, as if absorbing her into him.

She threaded her fingers through his short curls, wanting to feel him, needing to hang on for dear life as the boat churned on into the dark night.

Her dreams of him had never been this good.

She slid her palms lower to the corded muscle in his neck, the sexy ripple of his shoulders. His hands skimmed down her sides, sealing her to him with deft pressure. Her breast to his rock-hard chest, her belly to taut abs, her hips to the steely length of what she needed most.

"I want you, Nolee," he murmured against her neck between kisses. A shiver tore through her.

If she'd managed to keep Dylan at arm's length while on the trip, she might have been able to fight her own hunger. Could even have escaped this encounter if he hadn't opened himself up so completely to her. He'd laid himself bare and, in the process, laid her bare, too.

How could she not give in to each and every craving for him then and there? Indulge in her red-hot hunger for the rescue swimmer who could be on the next stateside flight and out of her life if she didn't grab her chance with him now?

Another time, she would figure out how to deal with a strictly physical relationship while they were on the boat. Later, after she'd had one more taste of Dylan's kisses, one more encounter with those expert fingers of his. As long as she kept her heart out of the equation, she could have this time with him and get him out of her system.

She'd worked so hard and played so little the last few months. Surely she deserved this small window of time to simply have fun.

Now or never.

She hadn't gotten to be captain of her own ship by questioning herself, by not taking chances.

She swung her leg over his and straddled his thighs. "I might have a few more tasks for you to complete, sailor," she murmured against his mouth. She felt the swell of his groin press hard against her buttocks.

His eyes gleamed and he raised his mouth so that his lips brushed hers. "I'm at your command."

DYLAN WRAPPED HIS fingers around the delicate curve of Nolee's neck and cradled the back of her head while her dark, fragrant hair spilled over his arm.

Sinking into the kiss, his eyes slid closed, too, his senses bombarded on every level. He needed to take his time. Concentrate. Appreciate every moment she allowed him to hold her this way.

And damn, was he appreciative.

He smoothed his hands down her tank top, then pulled it over her head and off. Coaxed by the thought of finally seeing Nolee's bare skin, he pried his eyes back open.

She stared down at him, naked except for black panties that shielded her sex. Her breasts swayed free, her curves supple and pale in the dim light of the stateroom. She looked like a damn fantasy.

Only he could reach out and touch. Taste. Explore even more.

His head was on fire with all the ways he wanted her. Banding his arms around her, he dragged her closer to kiss her harder, feel her. The lush press of her breasts against his chest, the warmth of her sex rubbing over his straining erection robbed him of air.

He broke the kiss to meet her gaze and she forced her eyes open with an effort, her long lashes fanning her cheeks. Air heaved in and out of his lungs, his chest rising and falling with the powerful effect of kissing her. Her mouth was swollen from his attention, her soft lips damp.

"Nolee," he breathed her name over her mouth, at a total loss for how to go slow with her. "You're driving me crazy."

"You're making me insane, too." She pressed her breasts to his chest, and the warm silk of her skin fried his brain cells, robbing him of any thought save having her.

All of her.

Sensation sent him careening headlong into a kind of sexual semiconsciousness, a realm where it was easy to forget everything else. At least until tomorrow.

He'd figure out a way to keep things simple later. For right now, he planned to give this woman everything in the world she wanted. Everything she deserved.

He lifted his face toward her breasts, gliding his lips across each curve with his tongue. She halted him with a hand on each cheek before he could reach the nipple and he straightened. Confused.

"Don't move." She used her fingernails to scrape down the front of his chest. It felt as if sparks flew from her touch, painting a trail of fire toward his—

She stopped too soon, teasing him with her exploring fingers a few inches above his waist.

He propped an eye open he hadn't realized he'd closed again, gulped for a breath of air and tried not to touch her. She needed, wanted to be in control this time and he could respect that.

He just didn't know if he'd survive it, or be able to scavenge any last bit of restraint. Sweat beaded his forehead and back.

She ground against his hardness before walking her fingers up his chest again.

Tension locked up every last inch of him. Maybe even a couple of extra inches, judging by the way his erection strained against her. "Honey, I don't know how much torment I can take. I've been thinking about you all week."

A wicked gleam lit her eyes. "Consider this an atonement for past sins. And some new ones I just might have in mind…"

He groaned at the thought of erotic anguish at Captain Nolee Arnauyq's hands. Not exactly a prison sentence, but another kind of torture. He promised himself he would let her have her way. He just needed one more touch of her first.

He clamped his hands on her hips and began to rock her, needing to feel the soft friction of her against his aching hardness. He slid her hips back and forth in a slow ride over his thighs. A torch lit up his insides, fanning a flame to billowing proportions.

Immediately he knew the movement had been as much

a mistake as a relief, because he only wanted her more, sooner.

Now.

"You've seen plenty of me," she said, gasping as he slid his finger inside the waistband of her panties and traced her anchor tattoo. "It's time you revealed a thing or two, officer. And I want the narrated version. Show and tell."

"You're turning into a force to be reckoned with, Captain," he growled.

A wicked smile played on her flushed face. "Let's start with the shirt, please."

He deposited her gently on the bunk then bolted to his feet. His balance tipped slightly with the heaving boat.

"Slowly," she purred once she'd stretched herself out along the berth, crossing her legs and resting her head in her hands, her brow knitting in mock concentration. "Did you ever see *Magic Mike*? Well. I loved that movie, and you're hotter than any of those guys. I want my own private show."

He nearly groaned out loud. The memory of every erotic combustible thing she'd ever let him do to her returned in a scorching rush.

"Are you sure? I'm going to make you want me pretty badly," he warned.

"Let's see what you've got." She shot him a knowing look.

Game on.

He tugged his tank from his waist, lifting it slowly, inch by inch, the cool air in the berth making his abdominal muscles contract. When the shirt reached shoulder height, he pulled it off and circled the fabric over his head before tossing it at her feet. One side of his mouth lifted.

There.

Nolee sucked in her cheeks, her look of approval filling

him with pleasure, strong and tart. Had she thought he'd back down? She was the one who'd been trying to remind him just how bold he used to be…not just when it came to saving lives, but in his own life, too. The one behind closed doors. How daring they both could be.

He unfastened his belt buckle then slowly slid the leather through the loops before dropping it to the floor. His fingers hesitated a moment above his straining zipper.

Go time.

He slid the iron teeth apart and pushed the fabric down over his hips, dropping his jeans so they pooled at his feet. The air slid across his bare ass and his rock-hard cock, her sharp intake of air the only sound in the room.

"Enjoying the view?" he asked, fairly sure it was a rhetorical question given the way her eyes roamed over his body, lingering on his bobbing erection, the shallow breaths coming from her parted lips.

"Get over here," she croaked, blinking fast, scooting forward to the edge of her berth.

He reached her in two steps and lifted her, squealing, against him. He turned in a circle, her thighs clenched around his waist, breathing in her mouthwatering, feminine smell. At last, he slid her down along the length of his body, hard and tight for wanting her.

"Is this what you want?" he growled once her toes grazed the swaying floor.

"Yes," she gasped, then she reached to a shelf behind him.

Sheathing himself in the condom she produced, Dylan forgot every reason he'd given himself to follow her lead and grabbed it himself.

Once he'd slid off her panties, he lowered himself back onto the bed, gathered her in his arms and positioned her over his lap, straddling him. Her thighs spilled over his so she was right where he wanted her. "I'm not nearly done with you yet," he vowed.

A fleeting smile danced over her mouth, eyes glittering with satisfaction. "If I had my way, you wouldn't be done for a very long time."

She made a show of sucking on her finger and then circled the tip of his cock with it. Teasing. His groin clenched in an agony of pleasure.

If he didn't give in to this insistent need soon, he'd explode.

Gripping her hips, he lifted her, savoring the feel of feminine flesh as he nudged his way past her entrance. The oceanic scent of her skin rose from her neck and shoulders to intoxicate him. He inhaled deeply.

Her eyes widened as he eased himself all the way inside, dark hair cloaking her tawny skin as she fell against his body. Something softened inside him at the way she gave herself to him, so totally uninhibited and unselfconscious. She was trusting in her complete submission, allowing him to take control.

Gone was Captain Arnauyq and in her place was Nolee, the woman who'd once rocked his world…still did. She trusted him enough to let down her guard. Unexpected tenderness threatened to level him as she wound her arms around him, holding on to him as if she wouldn't ever let go.

He didn't want to acknowledge the deepening, resurging connection he felt to Nolee, but it seemed suddenly to be there as naturally as his next breath. It went far beyond simply rekindling an old flame.

How had she justified trusting him again this way? And how the hell had he ended up thinking this now, when he was sliding between her thighs and the blood pounded through his ears louder than the swells outside?

But as her dark eyes looked into his, so giving and warm, he knew he would do everything in his power to make sure that trust of hers wasn't misplaced. She commanded him and he commanded her. It was a gut-check responsibility. Not one he would take lightly. Especially given his limited time in Kodiak. Nobody would hurt Nolee on his watch. Even him.

Especially him.

Then she cupped his face and kissed him, swiveling her hips, and all else was lost in a tide of pure sensation.

Except the need to imprint himself on her memory.

He gripped her hips, lifting her high so that he withdrew from her completely, and then he buried himself inside her all over again, hoping he could find the hedonistic rhythm that would make him forget all about this deepening bond he felt for her.

In a state of mental frenzy, he palmed her delicious ass and worked her hips to accommodate a faster pace, willing her to understand his need to forget. To lose himself in her. He thrust into her again and again, accelerating, faster, harder, nudging her to her own peak. Only when her back arched with a tension that gripped her whole body, her shrieks muffled against his mouth, her thighs squeezing his in a death grip, did he allow himself to hurtle over that edge with her.

Release came in one butt-kicking moment after another in a successive chain of spasms. He fell back onto the bed, Nolee in his arms. A primal satisfaction coursed through him long afterward, a pleasure that went beyond physical to a deep sense of rightness at being there with her. Too tired, too replete to question the feeling, he merely held her.

She dropped to his side and he cradled her in his arms. Within moments, her breath eased into an even rhythm, her eyes closed. Looking at her, he felt damn privileged to hold her. She was special. Unique. His first and only love. Not the kind of woman to be trifled with.

Yet he was in no position to offer her the serious relationship she deserved. Because as much as Dylan enjoyed his time with her, and despite their blazing reconnection, he knew he could never give up the nomadic lifesaving job that had always been his personal mission—not for any woman, even Nolee.

It was something she'd understood and accepted nine years ago, even before he had, when she'd let him go. The ultimate sacrifice. An act of true love. His heart clenched in his chest as he smoothed her hair. She would never leave this area, and he would never stay…

Could they enjoy each other now and walk away in a couple of weeks without looking back?

His eyes slid closed, and he rested his chin atop her head. Listened to her now regular breathing, his arms tight around her. One thing he did know was that he could not let her go.

Damned if he knew his way around their situation.

But he did know he wasn't ready for it to end.

Not now.

Not yet.

Maybe not ever.

11

NOLEE SLOWLY SWAM to consciousness, moored in Dylan's arms. A thick quilt enveloped them. It kept out the cool, damp air that flowed through the cracked-open porthole and protected the body heat that glowed inside their love nest.

Nestled against Dylan's steely contours, Nolee replayed last night's sensational sex. She squirmed backward and fitted her bottom snugly into the curve of his muscular side. Rock-hard arms tightened around her reflexively.

They'd vowed to make the most of their time together, enjoy one another physically while keeping things from getting emotional. She'd hoped that by taking charge last night, she wouldn't be as vulnerable. But the tenderness that now seized her, the sense of completeness she felt lying in his arms, as though a part of her, long missing, had just been returned to her, called into question all of her assumptions.

She might be older, wiser, but her heart had stayed constant, still opening for Dylan as easily as ever. It terrified her.

Returning to sleep was definitely out of the question.

A long, low ship horn reverberated across the sea. The

Pacific Dawn answered. Nolee slit open her eyes, hoping the day hadn't yet dawned. She wasn't ready to face last night's impulsive actions.

She took a fortifying breath of briny ocean air and peered around her. The world was gray and shadowed. Darn. Sunrise and reality were only moments away.

She thought about waking Dylan, leading him outside to share this sunrise the way they always used to, then stopped. She was getting way ahead of herself. They had less than two weeks until the opilio season ended and they went their separate ways.

How foolish to imagine, even for one unguarded moment, that they could have a second chance. They'd agreed that this could only be a physical affair. A time-limited, no-holds-barred, no-strings-attached sexual adventure, which should make her happy, but left her unsettled instead.

Dylan's deep breathing rumbled in his chest and vibrated against her back. She hated to wake him from such a peaceful sleep. They had another hard day ahead of them setting pots, and he needed this rest.

Hopefully, he'd keep sleeping so she could sort out her feelings. She inhaled his musky, masculine scent. The longer she lingered, the less clearly she could think.

A lonely rush of chilled air wafted over her as she emerged from his arms. Quickly she tightened the blanket around him. He stirred slightly, his arms reaching out into her now-empty space. A sigh escaped his parted lips, but he didn't wake. The hard planes of his face relaxed back into an impossibly handsome visage.

After dressing, she hurried outside to her favorite spot on the bow. Behind her, stacked steel pots rose twenty-five feet. They blotted out the wheelhouse, kept her from Stu's watchful gaze and gave her the privacy she craved to settle herself before she took the wheel for another fifteen-hour shift.

She took a fortifying breath of the briny ocean. In the distance, she spotted a large black ship with a distinctive motorcycle figurehead. Captain Bill's *Easy Rider*. Must be heading back to Dutch Harbor, she guessed, given its direction.

Her hair billowed behind her as she leaned against the rail. Across the semi-flattened arc of the horizon a glowing crack sheared into the dwindling dark as the *Pacific Dawn* drove through growingly rough seas. The sky was gray and oppressive, streaked with bloody orange trails, the low-hanging clouds full and purple tinged on the horizon.

A storm.

She didn't need a weather report to see the telltale signs of another gale. Her stomach churned along with the crashing swells, filled with uncertainty. Having Dylan on board had tipped the careful balance she'd made of her life. He was an exhilarating and generous lover, giving as much or more than he took. And what he gave…a shivering warmth rattled over her bones despite the frigid temperatures. He alone knew her body. How to make her scream with delight, writhe in exquisite agony. He could make her die slowly in his arms and then breathe life back into her with a single, searing kiss. He knew how to touch her in places no one else could.

What if her heart gave itself to him as easily as her body?

Her gloved fingers tightened on the rail. If she got too attached over the next two weeks, she'd be devastated when he left. She might not be able to let him go or worse…she'd be tempted to leave everything to follow him if he asked.

Please don't let him ask.

Boots clomped behind her. Nolee's back stiffened as she

was engulfed in Dylan's powerful embrace. He rested his head atop hers, pulling her close.

"Morning, beautiful," Dylan murmured low and husky in her ear, as if her thoughts had conjured him.

Heavy clouds blackened the horizon.

Nolee's traitorous heart drummed, nearly drowning out the rising waves.

"Looks like rain," she replied, concern rising. Lightning forked, an ominous rumble confirming her prediction.

"Red sky at night, sailors' delight, red sky in the morning, sailors take warning." He tossed out the old adage as he trailed a molten flow of kisses down her neck, wreaking havoc with her senses and her willpower, creating another kind of storm inside her.

It would be difficult to keep things light between them.

"Then you should be warned," Nolee managed, breathless from his touch. She twisted slightly around to peer up at him. "We'd better get going before the downpour arrives. Plus, someone might see us."

It was a weak objection, token really, since she made no move to step away. Couldn't if she tried, she admitted to herself. It felt perfectly right to be standing here with Dylan, the ocean at their feet, the rest of the world falling away.

"They're all snoring like logs." Dylan's devil-may-care smile flashed, as electric as the air crackling around them.

"Did Stu see you leave my room?"

"Nah." He shrugged, unconcerned. "I ducked outside while he was in the head."

"Good." She breathed out a relieved sigh.

"Ashamed of me?" Dylan eyebrows slashed downward, his inscrutable eyes narrowing, at odds with his teasing tone. He released her, then leaned his side against the rail. The wind ruffled his flattened curls and his nose flared.

"No. I don't want to give the crew any more reasons to doubt me."

"The crew adores you, Nolee."

Her lungs labored to push against the heavy weight now pressing on her chest. "I haven't made them any real money. That last haul was average at best, and we need to do better than that or we won't make quota."

Dylan squinted at the *Easy Rider*'s silhouette. "So call my uncle. Ask for help."

"No, I—I—can't." She clenched her teeth to keep them from chattering at a sudden, icy gust that whipped off the surf.

He gently raised her hood, then carefully fastened the Velcro closure. "Can't or won't?"

"Dylan, you know why I need to do this alone."

"I don't think I do, Nolee." His gloved hands slid down her arms to tangle in hers. "You never wanted to talk much about your life outside the ship back when we were together."

At the concern in his voice, her heart fluttered. She'd always been ashamed of her family's grinding poverty... had brushed it off, mostly, when she'd talked about it in the past. But suddenly she wanted to be real with him. Emotional currents pulled at her, sweeping her off balance, loosening her tongue.

"All my life I had to depend on others for everything. Where I would sleep, what I would eat...if I would eat." She shivered as she remembered nights she'd gone to bed hungry, questioning how much she mattered in a world that took hardly any notice of her, one where she made barely a ripple. "I promised myself I'd call the shots someday.

Control my life. Never go hungry or sleepless or without again."

"You could've stayed on the boat with me and Bill year-round, not just when we were fishing."

"No," she said fiercely. "Then I would've depended on you, too, and I couldn't have that. Never you."

He squeezed her hands then drew her close against him, smoothing a hand down her back. "Why, Nolee? What did I do to make you doubt me?"

She tensed against him and her gaze swept out over the horizon. "You're a man."

"And all men let you down," he prompted.

She opened her mouth to reply but the answer stuck in the back in her throat, swelled.

"You're talking about your dad."

Her eyes stung, and she turned around in his arms to face the brisk breeze stirring the waves. She shook her head fiercely. Denial.

"I don't care about him."

"Not even when you were little?"

Silence. Her breath rasped in her throat. Grated against the sandpaper of her tongue. In. Out. In. Out.

At last she said, "I wanted a PO box."

"Come again?"

"A PO box. I begged my mother to get one because we moved so much. I thought if my dad ever wrote me, his letter wouldn't reach me. If he ever came back for me, he'd never find me."

"Oh, Nolee…"

The break in his voice had her bracing. She wouldn't let anyone feel sorry for her. She was to be taken seriously. Respected. Not pitied. Not dismissed.

"It's okay. I mean, I knew he'd never come back for someone like me."

"What's that supposed to mean?" Dylan turned her so that they faced each other again, their sides against the bow. The sky drizzled, cold stinging sheets.

"I've never achieved anything, never done anything special with my life. I'm nothing. Nothing without…" She gestured, sweeping her arm out to encompass the entire deck.

"This ship? Your quota? Nolee. None of that defines you. And you mean a lot to many people. Especially me."

"Dylan. Don't."

"Don't what, Nolee?"

"Don't make me depend on you." Ashamed of her weakness, she stepped close and burrowed into him. Spoke into his chest. "Don't make me need you. Not again."

He smoothed a shaking hand over her hair. "I don't know how much of this I can control."

She pulled back. "Me, neither. And that scares the hell out of me. I'd better go and relieve Stu."

His eyes searched hers. "I'll wake the crew. Call my uncle, Nolee. It's not a weakness to ask for help. You're not the girl you used to be."

Pleasure ripped through her at his words. He was right. She wasn't that hungry, scared, powerless little girl anymore, forced to accept others' help. She decided when to reach out to others and right now, with her quota a dwindling dream, it was time to admit she couldn't do this alone.

"See you tonight," he whispered against her lips before capturing them in a head-spinning kiss. Then he strode across the slick deck and disappeared from view.

A half hour later, up inside the wheelhouse, Nolee picked up her handheld and spoke into it.

"Bill. Bill. Bill. This is Nolee—do you copy?"

After she repeated the question a few times, Captain Bill's voice sounded through the speaker.

"Nolee, this is Captain Bill, over. How the hell are ya, kid?"

She felt herself tighten, resisting what she was about to say. To admit.

"Not so good. Haven't found much crab. I'm—ahhh—wondering if you might have any leads on where they might be at."

In the ensuing silence, her palms grew damp.

"Yeah. Just set a town soak string right over a hot spot. Better haul ass and start mowing if you're gonna beat these other assholes that might be listening in."

"Thanks for the tip, Bill," someone else growled over the line. Jake Scanlon, the youngest and newest captain in the fleet. "What'd you say those coordinates were again?"

"Shove it, Jake."

Nolee grinned as she jotted down Bill's rapid-fire coordinates. "Roger that, Bill. And, thanks."

"Don't choke me down, Nolee," he added, referring to a practice less scrupulous skippers had of setting lines to prevent others from extending their run. "Or, Jake. Over."

She stopped herself midbristle, knowing he was only messing with her, and teased the crusty captain right back. "Maybe I will. Maybe I won't. Oh. And one more thing."

Nolee eyed the bustling crew below, her gaze lingering on Dylan. He'd admonished her that she wasn't her childhood self and neither was he.

He had unresolved issues here in Alaska, serious ones that included a secret even Dylan didn't know yet about his family, one his mother had insisted Nolee keep until she could tell him herself.

No matter what he said, or didn't say, he hurt over them…even if he couldn't admit it. She owed it to him to help him gain closure over this aspect of his life, before he left Kodiak. Although, technically, he hadn't mentioned his transfer papers in a while…was it possible he'd changed his mind?

She brushed off the tempting thought and asked, "Will you tell Dylan's mother he'll be at Chart Room Grill in five days if she still wants to meet with him?" They had their second offload date with the distributing plant and would have a one-night layover in town.

"Does Dylan know about this plan?"

"Not yet, but he will."

"You think he'll agree?"

"Let's just say, I might have some influence…"

"Roger that, Nolee. Bill, out."

Nolee settled the unit back in its holder and set her coordinates. Outside the wind chafed the surging sea and pushed back against the scuttling crew. Dylan stood tall, legs spread, body unbowed by the storm. He looked invincible, but she knew better.

She was taking a chance pushing this issue with Dylan, and he might not agree with her planned reunion. He'd be furious with her. Yet she sensed that part of his restless spirit would never be free of his past until she helped him resolve it.

As for herself…well…it seemed as though she only risked reopening old wounds by being with him. But she'd survived one morning after without falling hopelessly in love with Dylan Holt again.

Only fourteen more to go.

12

A FEW DAYS LATER, Dylan shook feeling into his numb hands and exchanged a grin with Nolee across the deck's tank chute. His heart thudded at the childlike delight on her face as if he was swimming in thirty-foot swells. The need to pull her into his arms and tempt her to his bed, ever present these days despite their grueling work schedule, hit him hard. He shoved down the driving impulse. With others around, he had to bide his time to get her alone.

Private moments had been frustratingly few and far between with the crew underfoot and Nolee working more on deck. Stu's arthritis had flared yesterday, and she'd swapped her longer shifts at the wheel to let him rest his joints.

"Tanks topped!" Nolee spun the hatch closed on their second full tank, bringing them closer to a million-dollar catch if they kept up these numbers.

"Boo-yah!" Tyler fist-bumped a grinning Jo then pulled back his hand, fingers spread wide.

Tim grabbed something invisible and thrust his hips forward, grinning maniacally. "Now that's what I'm talking about! Uh! Uh! Uh!"

Flint danced his trademark Krabby Patty jig. "We're rockin' and rollin', baby! Take me to the bank."

"Now put it back in with a bunch of bait," Nolee ordered the crew, teeth flashing, eyes sparkling. Dylan's breath caught. No woman had ever affected him this way. "We're offloading in ten hours."

Bill's tip had paid off big-time. They'd been running hard, working sixteen-hour shifts, hauling as much crab as possible before their looming offload date. They had to be at the heart of a mammoth school, or its leading edge, because the crabs were big and clean.

Seemed like they'd left their nail-biting days of grinding off zeros behind. Yet even these large numbers didn't make up for earlier setbacks. Nolee still worried, as did Dylan.

He'd been distracted, at least, when the old rhythms of fishing returned to him. It was exhilarating to labor on the Bering Sea again, surrounded by a rugged landscape more beautiful than any he'd encountered in his travels so far: the changing, volatile climate, the dramatic sunsets, the endless ocean. He'd missed his hometown, he realized, now that he'd seen more of the world. His time here didn't have to be the misery he'd imagined. How long since he'd fished? Hiked? Camped?

Suddenly he wanted to do the things that'd once seemed more like familial obligations. Most of all, watching Nolee, he wanted her as much as he ever had…maybe more. His emotions had deepened, fueled by the knowledge that she'd given up their future together so he could have his dream. Could he have it all, temporarily, and still walk away?

A SMALL EXPLOSION sounded off the starboard side and the entire boat vibrated. A shrilling note squealed through the pilothouse's glass. Nolee whirled from the launcher, her face stricken.

"What was that, Stu?" she called.

"We've got an issue in the engine room."

Nolee spun and Dylan sprinted after her and Wesley toward the engine room, his short hard breaths harsh in his ears.

"God damn it," he heard her swear before she flung herself through the hatch. He plummeted down the vertical ladder after her and yanked on a pair of the headphones they used to muffle the sound of the deafening engine. The cramped, humid room reeked of rust, sea water and oil.

"Which alarm is it, Wesley?" she demanded, squinting up at their pressure gauges.

"Over here." Wesley pointed at one of their engines. He'd pulled back the cover.

Dylan joined him, Nolee on his heels. He held his hand over it then yanked it back. "It's hot as fuck."

"Got to check the gearbox!" Nolee shouted and Dylan followed her to the apparatus.

Dylan scanned it, noting that the coolant wasn't reading. "It looks like it's seized!"

The noise of the engines was deafening, a never-ending timpani of thumping and grinding. It deluged the room, his ears, his head. He struggled to hear himself think even with the headphones on.

"Engine oil's down," Nolee canted, her features set. Fierce. His warrior-captain. "Jacket water's not registered. Nothing pumping for the starboard engine."

The boat lifted under them, sending all three staggering against the wall.

"Wow," yelled Wesley. "That's not good."

"No shit, Sherlock," Dylan ground out, his pulse slamming through his veins.

"All this vibration is coming from here." Wesley pulled

back the metal access and pointed at one of the gears in the starboard transmission.

They stared in horror. It was frozen, making it impossible for the engine to transfer power to the prop and push the boat forward.

"You can't fix a gearbox for a main engine at sea," Dylan thought out loud, then swore. "Son of a bitch."

Nolee relaxed her balled hands and met their gazes, her features set. Chin raised. She grabbed a radio set from its holder and spoke into it.

"Stu, do you copy?"

They strained to hear.

"Stu," Nolee repeated. Louder. "Stu, do you copy?"

After a static-filled pause, the answer came through loud and clear. "Stu here, over."

"We're down to one engine. It's going to be real slow going from here on out."

"We'll miss our offload time," Dylan heard Stu shout through the small speaker they now crowded around. "Do you want me to radio to reschedule? It'll be days…"

"We'll lose the crab." Wesley shook his head.

Dylan's jaw clamped tight. The extra time in the tank, waiting for the busy distributor to fit the boat in to offload, would kill off the crab; they'd lose their first solid take.

"Unless…" Nolee breathed a fast breath and her nostrils flared, her diamond stud flashing.

"Nolee…" he began, knowing that ferocious look on her face. It was the expression she wore right before she did something really, *really* risky. Every cautious bone in his body seized.

"Stu. Set course."

"Where?"

"False Pass."

Dylan's heart dropped. Damn it. Nolee knew better than

to take the treacherous shortcut. It'd save them time, if—
and it was a big if—they made it though. It cut too close
to the shoreline to be anything but a dangerous pass of
last resort. Seasoned captains had run their ships aground
there, lost their hauls in that dangerous, narrow and winding channel.

He opened his mouth to object and reason with her.
Better to risk losing their offload date and payoff than the
entire ship. Crew. But his lips clamped shut at her determined expression, and he followed her topside.

Real and present danger loomed, but it wasn't necessar-
ily a given. A skilled captain had a chance of pulling them
through, and Nolee, he'd come to learn these past couple
of weeks, was damn good behind the wheel.

Her claims of *I'll take care of it* weren't just talk. She
did take care of it. The sweat equity she put into the crew
and boat… It might make him lose sleep, but that same
daring, crazy, ferocious quality made her an outstanding
captain the crew was lucky to have. They respected and
trusted Nolee, and he should, too.

The Bering Sea would chew you up and spit you out.
As a skipper, you had to be able to hang and she'd proven
her mettle. She wanted, needed, *deserved* for others to believe in her and right now, that started with him.

Once on deck, she paused at the rail and stared out at
the rollicking, surging chop, the darkening line of clouds
on the horizon. Gulls circling the scene were shrieking.
He squeezed her waist. "You got this, Captain."

Nolee turned, as if brought back reluctantly from distant thoughts. "I'd better have it. Would you join me in
the pilothouse?"

"You couldn't order me away."

The staring, anxious crew filed into the galley after

them for their first break in nearly twelve hours. Nolee must be exhausted, too, but she didn't show it.

"Are we dumping the crab, Captain?" asked a muted-sounding Flint, his expression hangdog, his features falling in on themselves. He leaned, whey-faced, against the counter.

"Nah. We're taking a shortcut. False Pass."

Tyler whistled. "Ah, buddy. Knock 'em dead, Captain."

"Got it covered. Get some shut-eye. Everyone but Wesley. We'll be offloading in eight hours."

Upstairs, Stu vacated the captain's chair and Nolee slid behind the controls.

"Get some rest, Stu."

The older man crossed arms over a prominent belly and braced against the heaving boat. "I'm talking you through this. Looks like we got some weather coming in."

She shook her head. "That's an order. You've been driving straight for twelve hours. Your wrist is swollen as hell. Soak it in Epsom salt and get some sleep. Besides, I've got Dylan."

Nolee's eyes, when she looked at Dylan, were clear and steady, a rich brown. He nodded. If she was taking a risk, it wouldn't be alone. They had each other.

Always had.

Time, distance and heartbreak hadn't changed a single thing between them. Was he a fool for thinking he could leave her and Kodiak in just under a couple of weeks?

Damn straight.

But no time to think about that now, not with a disabled engine and an incoming gale degrading their already complicated mission.

Nolee wanted his support, wanted him, at least for now, and he'd make the most of every moment they had left... even this one.

He took his place at the windshield to call visual cues as Nolee steered the boat to the treacherous sea lane. Dylan stared out of the glass at the water heaving and churning around them, occasionally meeting the salt-stained windows with an emphatic slap.

"Don't worry, Nolee."

"Do I look worried?" She flicked him a quick look then peered back at her controls. Her dead-serious tone nearly made him laugh despite everything. Of course she wasn't anxious. She had him to do all the worrying.

And there was plenty to be concerned about.

"I'm down, but I'm not out," he heard her murmur under her breath. "I'm down but I'm not out."

He brushed a hand over the back of her head. "Nolee?"

"I've just got to start talking positive to myself," she continued as if she hadn't heard him. She edged up the throttle, pulled it back, her hand on the black joystick of the thrust. "I can do it with one engine."

He opened his mouth to object then shut it. Crab-fishing boats had twin screws and didn't function well on one engine. They were designed and made to run on two. Without both, they'd lose steering and speed. With half the horsepower, braving the narrow pass in stormy weather would test Nolee's skill and put the lives of the crew, as well as the boat and the lucrative catch, at risk.

"There's no reason I can't do this," she said to herself. "I don't want to hear any worst-case scenarios, okay, Dylan?"

He nodded. She was right. His brand of negative thinking had no place here. The time to second-guess was long gone. He squeezed her shoulder as Stu stumped downstairs to his berth, muttering warnings.

"You've got this."

She briefly placed a hand over his, then returned it to the controls.

Forty-five tense minutes later he spotted a bobbing red triangle. The silver-blue sea darkened to slate, muddied and swelled into threatening peaks. The winds, born as whispered breezes, grew to stiff gusts, then amplified to gale force, hurling javelins of rain. His heart rate quickened. "First marker. Port."

"Copy." Nolee maneuvered them past the first outer sandbar. "Race is on. It's going to be tight."

His pulse shot, rapid-fire, through his veins. If she missed even one marker, they'd run aground. She had to hug the winding, narrow route exactly, avoiding its shallow bottom while maneuvering through its weird currents and whirlpools.

No margin of error.

He pointed at the marine map. "The current flows right past here. And there's a sandbar. See that deep ditch?"

Nolee nodded and labored to steer with limited power. If she brushed up against the sandbar, the *Pacific Dawn* would start sucking sand up into the tanks, suffocating the crab.

"Want Wesley to turn off the pumps?"

"Not yet. I don't want to deprive the crab of oxygen until I absolutely have to."

He bit back his cautionary words again. Nolee had the right mindset for a commercial fisherman. Work like hell for a big payoff that profited the boat's owners, herself and her crew. Bring everyone and the vessel home safe.

Not the same point of view for a professional rescuer. Assessing life's potential dangers was automatic for him. He expected, prepared for, worst-case scenarios. Worked like hell to minimize or avoid them entirely. His life-and-death work required him to constantly weigh the odds and choose the safest route.

Not so for Nolee. She never flinched from rolling the dice.

But in some ways, he and Nolee had that in common. That night in the bar, she'd reminded him that they weren't so different. Both risk-takers. Both living dangerously. Both doing whatever it took to defy the odds.

Except when it came to one another.

Nolee squinted at her depth finder. The blue screen, punctuated with red to orange to yellow spikes, heralded dangerous fluctuations in depth. A large number flashed on the lower right corner of the screen.

Twenty-six feet. The *Pacific Dawn*'s flat bottom only gave them a ten-foot leeway. Sweat beaded on his brow; he tore his gaze away and studied the chop.

"It's getting nautical out here," Nolee muttered as she strove to harness her crippled boat. Beneath them, the ship bucked and rolled her way through the waves, groaning with the effort. "With one engine, she's going to do what she wants."

Twenty-two feet.

Several minutes ticked by. A half hour. Forty-five minutes. Time was marked only by the pounding of the seas, the periodic sounding of the depth reader, the incessant clanging of the metal chains outside.

The boat pitched violently. "This is getting worse the shallower we go," he said, widening his stance to keep his footing.

"A real washing machine," Nolee affirmed without looking up from the fathometer.

Twenty feet. The number blinked lower and lower. Eighteen feet. Seventeen.

"It's just going down," she gasped.

A channel marker loomed yards off the bow, catching his eye. His pulse slammed. The ship barreled right at it.

"Are we making the turn on the track here?" He pointed at it then whipped his head around to study her sharp profile.

"I'm trying." Her strained voice emerged through clenched teeth. She jimmied the thruster and peered up from her monitors and out the window.

The *Pacific Dawn* churned forward.

"She's just driving straight. She's not fucking turning."

Shit.

"Hang in there, Nolee," he urged. Helplessness crashed over him. He wasn't in control. Couldn't rescue everyone, including the ship and the catch. Couldn't get them all to safety. A damned unfamiliar feeling. But not entirely uncomfortable.

Why?

Because you trust her, came the sudden, unexpected thought. In fact, when push came to shove, he couldn't think of anyone else he'd rather have by his side in a situation like this than Nolee.

Could that extend to other parts of his life?

Dylan shifted his balance expertly as the floor rose beneath him and spray obliterated the view from the window. His gaze swung to the fathometer as it began beeping loudly.

Fifteen and a half feet.

Beeping. Thirteen.

Nolee shoved to her feet and snatched her walkie-talkie.

Ten feet.

Ten feet!

"Turn those pumps off, Wesley!" Nolee roared into her handset.

"Copy that, Captain." At the sound of the engineer's voice, Nolee dropped back into her seat and continued wrestling with the *Pacific Dawn*. "Come on. Turn!"

"Faster. Faster," someone chanted behind them and

Dylan pivoted to see most of the rest of the crew now bunched up behind them. They looked haggard and electrified, over-bright eyes in gray faces.

"Go. Go. Go!"

"Come on, turn!"

"One and a half million dollars," said Stu, pointing downward. "Right there."

"I'm going full steam," Nolee gasped and swiped at the sweat rolling down her brow.

White exhaust billowed from the stovepipe outside.

Flint stumped forward and peered over Nolee's shoulder at the odometer. "It's pegged!"

The *Pacific Dawn* couldn't go any faster. Would she turn aside in time before slamming into the sandbar?

Nine point eight!

Beep beep beep beep beep…beep…beep…beep… beep…

The vessel swerved at last with a grinding scrape and the shrilling depth reader gradually slowed. Then quieted. Dylan released a breath he hadn't known he was holding.

Ten feet. Fourteen. Twenty.

"Oh she's doing fine now," crowed Stu.

"Yeah! That's what Captain gets paid for," whooped Tyler.

"Nice," observed Jo, who set a water bottle beside Nolee.

"That wasn't fun for me, guys." Nolee's laugh shook slightly and then she lifted the water bottle and slugged back a long drink.

"Wow that dropped fast. When it got down to ten feet below the keel…" Stu shook his head. "That scared the shit out of me."

Nolee screwed the cap back onto her bottle. "Same,"

she admitted, then spoke into her handset again. "I think we can kick those pumps back on, Wesley."

"Sounds good to me, Captain. Over."

Stu clapped Nolee on the back. "Nice work and good luck through the rest of the pass. I'm hitting the rack."

The rest of the group vocalized their admiration then disappeared downstairs, leaving Dylan alone with Nolee.

The humming engine filled the sudden quiet.

"Good work, Captain," he rasped, then swooped down to plant a brief hard kiss on her mouth before he stepped back to his station at the window.

"Child's play," she bragged, her expression cocky as hell and so damn sexy. Hunger for her surged. She was such a mix of vulnerability and bad-girl attitude. He didn't think he'd ever get tired of exploring her contradictions. Inside *and* outside the bedroom.

"Oh, and Dylan? Thank you. I'm—uh—glad you're here."

It was at that moment, as he looked at her serious face, heard her admission and understood what it must have cost her to make it, that he knew his feelings for her could no longer be considered casual. Or simply physical. Or short-term.

"I—I—" The shock of this knowledge drove his voice from him, and he shook his head mutely. He found his thoughts suddenly, irrevocably, drawn to his upcoming transfer, and he felt exposed, flooded with regret.

"I—I'm always here for you, sweetheart," he said at last. The endearment stumbled off his tongue, as did a promise he wasn't sure he could keep.

But damned if he wanted to take it back.

She held his gaze for one more moment, then nodded before returning her attention to her controls. "Good."

Outside, the Bering Sea raged along with his thoughts.

He had no business making pledges like that. Not when his approved transfer papers probably awaited him in port. Yet quitting Kodiak no longer appealed to him.

He wasn't ready to leave Nolee just yet.

Logically, he knew it made the most sense for them to part ways at the end of the opilio season. Nolee never wanted to leave Kodiak and his career demanded that he travel. If she followed, she'd feel isolated, separated and stifled. And one day, she'd come to resent him.

But the idea of moving away bothered him now on a fundamental level. He'd never been the kind of person to start something he didn't finish. More than that, Nolee meant something to him…probably more than he cared to admit.

Was he being selfish by indulging in this short-lived affair? Neither one of them was cut out for casual. What's more, they had too much history to avoid going deep.

Yet just like the now-crippled *Pacific Dawn*, he couldn't easily navigate away from his feelings.

Or Nolee.

13

"YOU CLEAN UP NICE." A mischievous twinkle flickered in Dylan's gaze as they stopped at one of the Chart Room Grill's windowside tables the next afternoon. Outside, swirling snowflakes transformed Dutch Harbor into a snow globe. Powder-covered ship masts rose tall and stark white; church spires punctuating a gray sky.

Despite her bone-deep ache from offloading tons of crab last night and an equally strenuous, exhilarating night in Dylan's arms, her senses leaped wide awake. Her heart beat double-time at his flirtatious look and the sexy timbre of his voice.

His big shoulders angled over hers as he pulled out her chair, drawing his chest into agonizingly touchable range. She remembered how it felt to be crushed up against his solid, unyielding body. She wanted nothing so much as to put herself there again, and forced herself to sink into her seat to put distance between them.

How could she respect the boundaries in a no-strings-attached relationship when they were together all the time? When she wanted him every minute of it!

Besides, she had much more serious plans for Dylan than hauling him back to her stateroom for another steamy tryst. His mother was waiting in town to meet with him, and Nolee had to convince him to see her.

"You're not so bad yourself," she drawled. It was a vast understatement. His curls had grown out enough to swirl over his brow and flip above the tips of his ears, the ends damp from a recent shower.

His sculpted face, rugged and sun-darkened, dragged the air clean out of her every time she looked into those emerald eyes. In a body-hugging red thermal shirt and fitted jeans, he'd never looked more handsome.

"Not *so* bad?" Dylan asked, dubious, amused, one side of his gorgeous mouth lifting. He slid into the chair opposite hers and arched a brow.

She buried her nose in the menu. Peeked over the edge. "Stop staring," she chided, unravelling at the steady heat in his eyes, the way his boot tip slid over her ankle beneath the table—back, forth, back, forth. Her body revved.

"Good afternoon," chirped their waitress. She set down two filled water glasses. "Do you need a few more minutes to look at the menu or do you know what you want?"

Dylan's nostrils flared. "I know what I want," he said without taking his eyes off Nolee. Then, "Ouch!"

He reached down to rub the spot she'd kicked and she grinned to herself. "I'll just have coffee, thanks."

"And you, sir?"

"Hydrocodone and shin guards."

"Excuse me?" The waitress lowered her notepad. A line formed over her nose, bisecting her brow.

Dylan waved a hand. "Forget it. Coffee and…" He paused then asked Nolee, "Don't you want anything to eat?"

She twisted the napkin she'd dropped in her lap. "No. I thought we could talk first."

He snapped his menu closed and set it back on the table. "We'll keep these for now then, thanks."

The waitress bustled off at his words.

Dylan reached over the table to take Nolee's hand in his, rubbing his thumb in lazy circles on the inside of her wrist. Her flesh tingled, trembled and tightened where Dylan touched her. Heat pulsed through her legs, making her glad she wasn't on her feet. She wouldn't trust herself to stand with her muscles melting at his caress.

"What'd you want to talk about?"

Reluctantly, she pulled her hand from his. "Someone might see us."

He surveyed the room, skeptical. "This isn't exactly a sailors' hangout."

She took in the carved light fixtures, the gleaming tiled floor. "True."

"So who's the mystery guest you told me to dress nice for? Am I going to meet your mother at last?"

"*A* mother, anyway."

His grin faded slightly. "What do you mean?"

Spit it out, girl.

"I invited Marlene to join us."

The skin around his tightly clamped mouth whitened. He blinked at her, then shoved back his chair and stood.

"I'll see you on the boat."

She wrapped her fingers around his strong wrist. Dylan twisted back to face her.

"Please, Dylan. Just hear me out."

A muscle in his jaw jumped.

"Please."

"What time is she getting here?"

Nolee pulled out her cell phone and waved it. "She's just waiting for me to call."

Dylan leaned back in his chair and crossed his arms over his chest. "Five minutes. Then I'm outta here, Nolee."

Five minutes to undo decades' worth of pain? Not happening. But maybe, if she could loosen up his resistance a little, it would give his mom an opening to get through to him. She might not ever have closure on her issues with her father, but Dylan…he had a chance she'd never get, and she wouldn't let him squander it.

"Four and a half minutes," Dylan said, glancing at his watch.

"Oh. Thanks." Nolee accepted the mug of coffee the waitress set in front of her and lifted the pungent black brew to her mouth. Blew on it.

Stalled, basically.

Weighed her words.

She had to get this right. Tread carefully.

"Dylan. You're an ass." She winced as she sipped her scalding coffee.

There. Just the right amount of delicacy needed to get through to this thick-skulled knucklehead.

"If this is your idea of therapy, don't quit your day job." His quirked mouth took the zing out of his statement.

"How are you ever going to figure things out with your family if you're always running away from them?"

"You've got that backward. Remember? They were the ones never around."

"Yes. But I'm not talking about them. I'm talking about you." She blew the curling steam off the surface of her brew and drank again.

He was quiet for a minute, then, in a voice ragged with emotion, said, "So I'm to blame for them not caring enough to want to—oh—I don't know…raise their child?"

"No. That's on them. All I'm saying is that you can

only control you. Stop shutting people off, turning your back on them."

A gust of arctic air blew inside with an arriving family. They gathered at the hostess station, stamping feet and rubbing gloved hands.

"I don't..." He closed his mouth as she stared him down, eyebrows raised. "Fine." He let out a breath. "With you. And I was wrong to do that. But them... Come on, Nolee. You know how they are."

"No, I don't know how they are." Well. She did know one thing Dylan didn't know, and damn it, he needed to stay here and listen to what his mother had to say. "And I'm not turning my back on them without considering every angle, like you do."

"But I don't..." He swore under his breath at her steady look. "Okay. Guilty."

"Stop distancing yourself from emotionally challenging times. Face your mother. Hear her out."

He glanced down at his watch. "Time's up."

She bit her lip. Shook her head. "I'm on your side, Dylan."

"It's not looking that way, sweetheart."

"Maybe not. But I am. Your mother loves you. And your father, too. He's counting on you seeing him. It'd mean a lot to him."

She didn't dare say any more about his father in case she spilled a secret she'd promised to keep. But Dylan really needed to know...

"Right."

"They do," she insisted. "Every time I run into your mother she's always bragging about you."

He sputtered on his drink. Set down the cup. "You're talking about my brother."

"Nope. Not unless he joined the Coast Guard and rescued six from a sinking ferryboat during a hurricane last year."

He angled his head and his narrow-eyed gaze roamed the wall over her shoulder. Behind her, a child began to fuss.

"And where did she say that happened?" he asked, dubious.

"In Saint Thomas. Said you got the medal of honor. Showed me a clipping from…what was the name of that paper?" She tapped her chin then snapped her fingers. "The *Daily Advantage*."

"The *Daily Advance*?" His voice, when it emerged, sounded as though he'd strangled it.

"Yeah. That's what I said."

"It's the local paper in Elizabeth City, North Carolina. My last assignment before here. How did she have it?"

"Well. You know. We do get mail once in a while, even if we live at the end of the world." She settled back in her chair, extended her legs and crossed one ankle over the other. "Maybe she subscribes."

Dylan leaned forward and dropped his elbows on the table. His steepled fingers concealed his mouth and the tip of his nose. "But why…?"

"Gee," she shrugged, trying hard to keep her tender concern from showing too much. Dylan needed tough love. Maybe a kick in the ass, too. "I don't know…seeing as she has absolutely no interest in you. Not to mention that you're irritating as hell."

"Huh."

Despite her best efforts to stay tough, a tear nipped the corner of her eye as she watched Dylan grapple with this contradictory portrayal of the family he'd thought didn't care.

"Just hear her out, Dylan. For me."

"Okay," he said after a long minute. "But next time, you're the one lying on my couch, doc."

"Will I have to get naked for that exam?" She batted her eyes.

He sucked in a fast breath. "I intend to be quite thorough."

She shivered at the sizzling promise in his eyes. Downed a final gulp of her coffee and licked her lips. "Then I'll see you on the boat."

"Naked," he called after her, loud enough to make the wailing baby hush and a waitress bearing a drink-laden tray halt.

"With bells on," she replied, laughing, then blew him a kiss before slipping out the door.

After signing off with Dylan's delighted-sounding mother, Nolee wandered down to the dock. Heavy snow drifted from the leaden sky, catching on her eyelashes, the tip of her nose. She pulled up her scarf and thrust her gloved hands inside her parka.

Had she gotten through to Dylan?

For his sake, she hoped so.

After meeting with his mom, maybe he'd stop making quick judgments and begin to see that there were more sides to every story, every issue, than just his own.

She stopped to lean against the railing of a small footbridge and watched a laboring crew chip ice off their lines.

Her father had been a crab fisherman, her mother once told her...one of the rare times she'd divulged anything about the man who'd abandoned them.

Her cousins had called him a magician. When she was born, he'd simply disappeared, they'd joked. Her chest squeezed at the memory of her laughing relatives. She'd joined in with them then, telling herself she didn't care, but she did, she saw now. Still.

Very much.

Her fingers tightened on the slick rail as a sense of vertigo twisted through her. An endless fall.

Dylan had run away from his family. Her? She'd stayed put. But those weren't two different things after all. She'd avoided her father, too. Her mother had said she hadn't stayed in Kodiak for a love of the place.

Could she mean that Nolee stayed here because of her father? A crab fisherman. Was it possible she'd gone into his profession wanting to show she was worthy? Not someone to be rejected, dismissed?

She'd always hoped he'd find her someday, but why hadn't she ever thought to go find him?

Fear.

Fear of rejection, came the swift, hard answer. Her father's rejection had made her feel as though she wasn't good enough. That the outside world would judge her and find her lacking and unworthy, too. Perhaps she needed to reevaluate.

Who was she working so hard for? Pushing to be such a young captain for? Taking chances, as Dylan pointed out? Perhaps she'd been trying to prove herself to a father who had no relevance in terms of who she really was.

She resumed her walk, her boots tracking through the accumulating snow. If she was wrong about her father, she might also be mistaken about Dylan. Hadn't she been as guilty as he was in making snap judgments without thinking things through?

Her actions weren't selfless when she'd let him think the worst of her and Craig. In fact, looking back, she'd been protecting herself, trying to bring about what she thought was inevitable so it wouldn't take her by surprise—being hurt when he left her, just like her father had.

If she'd let go of her fear, they might have had a long-distance relationship. He wasn't like her father and she should have opened up to him.

Maybe it wasn't too late.

The biggest risks she'd taken were the ones involving her heart, she now saw…and falling…well…it wasn't the worst thing.

Not even close.

She couldn't lose everything when she still had herself.

"I'M SORRY, DYLAN."

Dylan stared at his mother, listened to her voice, but couldn't quite see or hear her. Somewhere far away, he thought he heard himself say, "Water under the bridge."

Wiry gray strands now threaded her frizzy brown hair. The lines around her eyes now furrowed deeply into her weathered skin. Years of squinting at the sun, at a summit, down a white-capped river, time leaving its mark.

But not him. Had he disappeared from her life without a ripple? He'd believed it for ten years, but now he wasn't so sure.

When she reached across the table for him, he dropped his hands and clenched them in his lap.

A sigh escaped her lips. "I made a lot of mistakes. Your father, too."

"No one's perfect," muttered the stranger who'd hijacked his mouth.

She raked a hand through her hair. The familiar gesture tugged at his heart—or it would, he guessed, if he could actually feel anything right now. Which he couldn't.

Wouldn't.

"Please give me more time to explain. Come home for a meal. It'd mean a lot to Robbie." She paused, then continued in a thickened voice, "Your father, too."

A bitter laugh escaped Dylan as the war zone of his childhood closed in. Rapid-fire memories peppered him. His sixteenth birthday.

EIGHT AT NIGHT. Infield. Bone-tired after losing in two extra innings. No going home. No cake. Not until he'd fielded fifty ground balls hit by his father.

"Your error cost the team the game," he hollered. "We're working on your fielding, so you don't let others down."

"You're a bastard!" Dylan yelled, contemptuous, then ripped off his glove and stormed away.

HE SHOULD HAVE been happy when his parents accepted his uncle's offer of a place to stay on his boat.

Shouldn't have been surprised when they'd stopped attending his games, swim meets…even his graduation.

He'd never spoken to his old man again.

He lifted a water glass and drank, giving his memories time to recede before saying, "That's doubtful."

"Honey. It's true." A tissue fell apart in her twisting hands, the white snowing on the blue table linen. "I wish your dad were here to tell you this, too."

Old resentment rose. "So why isn't he here to yell at me himself?"

Seemed logical to him. No one relished telling Dylan how he fell short more than his father. He'd rammed it down Dylan's throat every day of his life.

She squeezed her eyes shut and said, "He can't."

Dylan tore off a chunk of bread from the basket and popped it into his mouth. "Why's that?" he asked after he'd finished chewing. "Is he climbing the Himalayas? Blindfolded? Barefoot?"

She opened glistening eyes. "Will you please come? You're his son."

"I was his recruit," Dylan spat. "Not his son."

"Whatever else you believe about him, he's always loved you," his mother said, face pale. "Please. Please come. If for no other reason, do this one thing for me. It's all I'll ever ask of you. I promise."

He took a ragged breath. Then another. And another. Unfurled the hands clenched in his lap.

"I'll think about it." He nearly whipped his head around to see who the hell had said that. Not him. Not in a million years. Though given the beaming look on his mother's face it appeared he had.

"When will you let me know?"

"Soon," he hedged, wanting to delay, cancel. Take it back. Shit. What the hell had Nolee gotten him into? Another evening applauding his brother's achievements and getting his ass handed to him by his father. "I'll call you next week."

"Thank you, sweetheart," she said later when she gave him a goodbye hug out in the parking lot.

Several hours later, Dylan strode down the hall of the USCG Kodiak air station to check in on his transfer request and swap his clothes for fresh laundry. A couple of servicemen scuttled out of his way and snapped to attention as he barreled down the hall. His boots rang on the polished floor and the familiar aroma of military wafted through the space: polish, disinfectant, freshly laundered uniforms. Compared to the salty, fish-scented Bering Sea air, it smelled sterile and stale. Life on half power.

No denying he wanted to get back to the crab boat and Nolee.

How would she react when he told her the news?

And why hadn't he shot down his mother's invitation?

Sure, he hadn't wanted to hurt her feelings. But that wasn't the whole truth.

You want to go.

He slung his repacked duffel higher on his shoulder and picked up his pace.

No. Yes. Maybe.

He hadn't a fucking clue.

Glutton for punishment.

And curiosity.

Nolee had raised too many questions—he couldn't leave Kodiak without having them answered.

Had he been wrong about his family all this time? If so, what did that mean about everything else he'd assumed about his life…himself?

"Sorry," he muttered as he sidestepped a clerk bearing a foam tray laden with sandwiches.

No doubt about it, Nolee had a point. After talking to his mother, he saw that he did push people away. Turned his back rather than faced his problems.

As a rescue swimmer, he didn't hesitate to fling himself physically into treacherous situations. But emotionally, Nolee was right, he backed off.

Detachment was a necessary evil in his profession. It got you through a mission. A day. A crisis.

But life?

No.

It was a damned bad policy to follow personally.

"Holt!"

He whirled and saluted. "Captain Barrie."

"At ease, son. Haven't seen much of you lately."

"Leave, sir. Crab fishing."

His commander scrunched his grooved forehead. "Thought you couldn't stand Alaska. Would have figured you for Turks and Caicos."

Dylan bit back a smile. "Maybe next time, Commander."

"Yes. Well," his superior harrumphed, ever awkward in conversations that lasted more than a couple of sentences. "Just finishing up our audit. Your rotation request is next on my list. Heard there may be an opening in Cape Cod. If it's true, they'll need a replacement."

A curious locking sensation snapped through Dylan's joints. "Good to hear, sir," he said through tight lips. His heart thumped sluggishly. A funeral march.

His commander stared at him curiously for a moment, inclined his bald head and turned on his heel.

"Dismissed, Petty Officer," he barked over his shoulder, then pushed through the opaque glass door to his office suite.

Dylan stared at it long after it'd swung shut.

Move your ass.

He resumed his trek.

Walk. Don't think. Walk.

Because suddenly he didn't know what to think. Or didn't know what to think of his thoughts.

Right then, when his superior had mentioned his transfer being delayed because of the audit, he'd been happy.

He'd wanted to call it off.

For Nolee.

The way she'd called him out about his own family hang-ups had made his feelings for her run deeper than ever. She knew him better than anyone. Better than he knew himself. Suddenly he wondered if he could survive without her.

He shoved through the side doors and the immensity of the dark, snow-filled sky seemed to press on his head. A throbbing flared behind his right eye. The beginning of a headache. After pulling on his knit cap, he headed back down to the ferry that would take him to Dutch Harbor.

The *Pacific Dawn* cast off tomorrow morning. Their last run of the opilio season. Just one more week with Nolee. Would it be enough?

No. He wouldn't leave her easily.

But what was the alternative?

Beneath the overhang in the passenger waiting area, he dropped his duffel and leaned against the particleboard wall. A ray of electric light zoomed in a semicircle over the rippling black harbor. The crying of the gulls was drowned out by a foghorn's blare. His chest fell as he exhaled a plume of white.

Should he consider staying in Alaska after all? He wouldn't be happy here, but he wouldn't be happy without Nolee, either. Perhaps he should rescind his rotation request.

He cared about Nolee, but were those feelings strong enough to settle his restless nature? He wondered if he could lay his head down in the same town every night. Stop wandering. Have that hearth and home and family he'd never believed he could have before because of his dangerous, demanding career.

Because you grew up thinking you weren't good enough. Didn't believe you deserved them...

With Nolee, it suddenly seemed possible.

Then again, even if he was willing to settle, would Nolee want him?

After she'd opened up about her missing father, he'd understood why she didn't want to depend on a man. Even if he stayed, she wouldn't want a serious relationship.

And that was for the best.

Wasn't it?

14

"ICE SALE. Ice sale today. Everything must go," bellowed Dylan in a ballpark barker voice.

He winked and Nolee's heart tripped over itself at the warmth in his teasing eyes. Then he hefted a large sledge-hammer and smashed it against the frozen launchpad.

Bam!

Crystal sparks glittered in the morning's arctic air and an ice chunk crashed to the slick deck. Over the rail, the frigid Bering Sea roiled and gulls wafted atop a harsh northerly blow.

Nolee stabbed at the crane's foot-long icicles with her pick, flexing her knees to keep from pitching with the ship, and rolled her eyes at his antics. "The weather forecast today? Pain," she announced in a huff of white air.

"No pain, no gain," Dylan interjected.

Despite temperatures hovering in the midtwenties, and the growing ice floe they'd battled for the past couple of days, Dylan looked unruffled. In fact, the high color in his cheeks and the sparkle in his eyes made it seem like he relished this extreme weather. A born and bred Bering Sea badass…

Like all of them, she thought, eyeing her mostly rookie

crew. They'd labored around the clock, setting and hauling pots while chipping at the unrelenting ice. Veterans didn't work any harder and she couldn't be prouder.

Or more grateful.

They were the reason she now hovered within striking distance of reaching her quota.

Not long ago, she would have resisted feeling dependent on others, but her first venture as captain had taught her how dangerous that line of thinking could be. Pride and insecurity never steered you in the right direction.

Once, those hang-ups drove her away from Dylan. She slid a sideways glance at the laughing, handsome man as he joked and labored beside the crew.

Could she—should she—seize this second chance to do things differently?

Her emotions for him delved deeper than physical. They even eclipsed her old feelings. Did she dare call them what she suspected…love? Dylan had broken through every last one of her defenses and now, with their time together about to end, she hadn't a clue what to do about it.

"It's stupid cold out here." Tyler bounced on the balls of his feet and shook his hands. He powered up the chisel again with an ear-splitting whine and raked it over the frozen railing.

"Not fit for man nor beast," Flint shouted. He blasted blue-red-orange flames with his blowtorch, melting the clear coating encasing the winch gears. "Ice a-comin'!"

Wesley and Jo exchanged a silent, tense look and Nolee rushed to reassure them about the worsening weather. "We've got time for one more hit. We'll bang that last tank out and put a lid on it."

She forced a confident grin, despite her reservations. According to this morning's ice report, the leading edge of a seven-hundred-and-fifty-mile-wide, two-foot-thick ice pack was descending on their fishing ground. The race was on to load the boat before the area froze over. And she sure as hell didn't want to be caught in it. Ice was like a great white shark swimming out on the horizon, just beyond your view. Unpredictable and deadly if you weren't watching.

She stared at the ice chunks bobbing on the swelling ocean. As long as the weather held, they'd have just enough time for this final haul. If the numbers remained steady, she'd make the quota she needed to secure her captain status with Dunham Seafoods, her future...everything she'd dreamed of.

With Dylan on board, however, assailing her body and her heart, battering down her defenses, she'd begun questioning if that was all she really wanted anymore.

But what else could she have?

Dylan?

He'd been noncommittal about going through with his family's invitation to dinner. If he avoided them, he'd never resolve his past bitterness and would leave Kodiak. On the other hand, he hadn't mentioned his transfer when he'd returned from his air station last week. Seemed like he should've heard something by now; he'd put in for it over a month ago. Perhaps, after reconnecting with Kodiak, and her, he'd had second thoughts and considered staying after all.

Maybe she just needed to give him a very good reason to stay.

Her lips curled as she thought of every steamy, naughty act she'd commit to persuade him the next time they were alone...

A few hours later, the group crowded in the warm galley, stacking their lunch dishes in the sink.

"All right, crew!" Nolee snapped off the faucet and

turned around. "You'll be down a hand, since I'm reliev-ing Stu so he can take a nap. Let's make this last string our best. Everyone stay safe. No accidents. Big money."

"Let's do this!" Tyler led the charge to their water gear and back out into the elements.

"Captain Bill's on the radio asking for you, Captain," Stu said through a yawn as he tromped down the pilot-house stairs. "Asked for Dylan, too," he added, then dis-appeared into his stateroom.

The portal shut behind the group with a wet gust, and Nolee and Dylan jogged upstairs.

On the landing, he pulled her into his arms and lowered his mouth. "Nolee." He breathed her name like an invoca-tion. "I can't keep my hands off you."

"Good."

He stopped her laughing response with his mouth. The brush of his lips electrified her, sending her pulse into a skidding frenzy. She savored the sweet point of contact as he kissed her thoroughly, deeply, passionately, the way she'd been wanting him to all day. He threaded his fin-gers through her hair, tilting her head back as his lips ca-ressed hers.

He tasted like peppermint, smelled like fresh winter sea air. She couldn't get enough, she thought, burrowing into his unyielding chest. His T-shirt grazed hers, broadcast-ing his taut body's heat and making her thoughts scatter as her hands slid around his waist.

The radio squawked and they froze. Dylan's ragged breath mingled with her shallow gasps as they eased apart.

"Captain Bill for Captain Nolee. Come in, Nolee."

With a groan, she flung herself into the chair, flustered, and snatched up her handset.

"Nolee for Captain Bill. Can you hear me? Over."

She stared at the icy spray that coated her salt-streaked

windows and tamped down the jittering, pulsing heat Dylan had ignited.

"Yeah. I've got you fine." Captain Bill's voice boomed through the airwaves. "Have you seen the latest ice picture? NOAA's got an update."

Her eyes flicked to Dylan. He'd joined her at the controls, and his rugged profile seemed turned to stone as he stared at the GPS screen. "Uhhhh. Noooooo. I've been working on deck. Not sure if Stu would have thought to phone NOAA again since we got their morning report."

Dylan dropped his hands to her shoulders and squeezed, his warm touch easing the concern now forking inside her.

"It's pretty much gonna be right across the 58 line from 172–173."

She frowned at her GPS map, and her heart sped up a beat. "So it'll be hitting where we are tomorrow morning?"

"Yeah," affirmed Captain Bill. "Friggin' scary."

Bill…afraid?

"That's a good pot!" she heard the crew exclaim outside and she watched, her gut twisting as they brought in another tank-busting haul. They couldn't leave now with the fishing this good.

Yet if Bill was right, she'd risk everything by staying.

"It was so far away." She passed a worried hand over her brow.

Dylan moved close and spoke into the handset. "Didn't think we'd have to worry about it for another couple of days."

"Yeah, the game is changing, bud. As we speak, we're worming our way down south back to port, so…"

Captain Bill had pulled up stakes and left this lucrative streak? As the toughest seadog in the fleet, that said a hell of a lot. None of it good.

Nolee blew out a long breath. "All right, Bill. Catch you later."

"Yeah roger, roger."

Silence descended as she settled the handset back in its cradle. "This morning's report said the ice was going to be on the 58 line the day *after* tomorrow."

"Where are we at right now?" Dylan asked, his voice grave. Heavy.

They studied the updating onscreen map.

"Probably 58-0-3."

"Shit." Dylan's jaw clenched.

"That's maybe 15–17 miles per hour faster than forecast." She lifted her hair off the back of her neck, her body clammy despite the frigid air.

Dylan frowned. "This changes everything. We've got a hundred and eighty-six pots left out here. The ice pack's going to cover them."

He pointed at her plotter, a screen that registered all the markers set and inputted into the system by the fleet. Her lines glowed blue and much farther north than the others, she noticed. "Not only will you lose crab, but you'll lose pots."

"Fourteen hundred bucks a pop," she muttered, her thoughts racing, stumbling over one another before any finished.

Dylan squatted beside her chair. Gathered her hands in his. "Nolee. We've got to get out of here."

"If we had two more days without this ice…" she groaned, her heart aching. Everything—every single thing she'd worked all her life to prove, was slipping out of her grasp.

Should she cut her losses and yank up the crabless tanks or remain and go for it? Ice reports, like storm predictions, had a margin of error.

Not a big one, though…

"But we don't have two more days. Twelve hours, max." He pulled her to her feet then turned her toward the windshield.

Outside, a growing number of ice chunks swirled and gathered atop the gray sea. When she shivered, he pulled her back against his muscular length and wrapped his arms around her. "What's your call going to be?" he murmured, his breath warm in her ear. "Captain."

The quiet assurance in his voice rattled through her. A seismic shift. Dylan knew she'd do the right thing. And so did she.

She caught a glimpse of her drawn face in an angled side mirror and raised her chin. If she lingered, she risked the ice engulfing her pots, losing money for the company and her chance at ever commanding another ship. Worse. She'd endanger the crew. If she left early, without giving her pots the time they needed to soak and catch crab, she wouldn't fill her quota.

Staying kept open the possibility of proving herself. Keeping her captain status with Dunham Seafoods.

Leaving meant… It meant that maybe she really didn't have anything to prove.

She met her eyes in the mirror again. Felt Dylan's heart drum against her back. Heard the steady rise and fall of his breath as he waited. Believed. Trusted that she wouldn't let him down.

She wouldn't let either of them down.

After all, who did she need to prove herself to? Not Dylan. He cared about her just as she was and so should she.

Ultimately, the only person she needed to answer to was the person she faced in the mirror. She pulled down the gooseneck mic and took a deep breath. "Crew. Crew. Crew."

Dylan ran his hands up and down her arms.

When the group stopped working to listen, she continued, "We just got a new ice report. Just revised. It's moving a lot faster than they predicted so we're going to pick up the gear and move off the grounds."

A round of swearing rose off the deck and she grimaced at the disappointment on their faces. Of course they wanted to make the maximum they could on this haul, but she wouldn't put their lives in jeopardy. She'd nearly sacrificed herself and the crew on her first boat when she'd played the odds and lost. This trip, this crew and Dylan had taught her so much about evolving, not only as a woman, but as a captain, too.

"We're going to pick up the rest of this string and stack the pots back up as we go. I repeat. We're not setting them back. Over."

"Copy that, Captain!" hollered Stu.

Dylan turned her around in his arms and brushed her hair from her cheeks, his touch gentle, the tender look in his eyes making her heart swell.

"I'm proud of you, Nolee." At the rich timbre of his voice, she felt her knees wobble, but she kept her back straight.

"So am I."

After a brief, heart-stopping kiss, he raced back out on deck to coordinate their hasty withdrawal. She closed her eyes for a moment and pictured the thousands of uncaught crab they'd leave behind. Her mother's admonishment whispered in her ear…the words of her people. Take only what you need. Her lashes rose and she peered down at the vibrant, larger-than-life man who'd rescued her when she hadn't wanted to be saved.

Who helped her when she'd wanted to go it alone.

Who made her depend on him in a way that made her stronger, she saw now, not weaker.

Why?

Because she loved him.

Always had. Always would.

Whatever the risks, the odds, she'd open herself up, surrender to her feelings and pursue what she needed most of all.

Dylan.

"LATER, DUDE!"

Dylan returned Tyler's wave from the dock, clapped Tim on the shoulder, then returned Jo's bear hug. Out on the horizon, the last of the sunset melted into a puddle of shimmering red-gold ripples atop the calm Bering Sea. The dark silhouette of a freight boat glided past, exhaling a long low note through the chilly air. Overhead, stars glimmered faintly in the purpling sky.

"Can't say I'll miss ya," cackled Flint, extending a hand.

Dylan grasped the older fisherman's hand and pumped it up and down. "Same," he agreed, not meaning it at all.

He'd enjoyed this motley crew, he mused, watching Flint and Tim barrel across the gangway to join Tyler and Stu. The group's full-throated laughter receded as they headed down the dock in the direction of The Outboard. After grueling weeks at sea, they would be eager to cut loose and spend some of their earnings.

The ragtag group had weathered their first opilio season and deserved some R & R.

As did Nolee.

She might not have met her quota, but she'd still done a hell of a job and deserved to celebrate. His groin tightened as he envisioned every decadent way he planned on making tonight special…for both of them.

He'd hardly laid eyes on her over the past couple of days as they'd worked nonstop to beat the ice floe and return safely to port. After grabbing a few hours of shut-eye, they'd offloaded while Nolee met with the distributors. She'd been huddled in the wheelhouse, doling out each fisherman's take since supper.

The last two hours he'd spent waiting for her had seemed to stretch into days. He'd spent most of it figuring out what he'd say now that the season had ended.

Not goodbye.

He wasn't ready for that yet.

Wesley appeared on deck, his tweed coat pockets bulging, his smile even bigger. "Solvency, here I come," he crowed. He slung an arm around a startled-looking Jo and planted one on her.

Her mouth opened and closed like a beached fish when he released her to shake Dylan's hand. "It's been a pleasure, sir."

"Mine, too."

"I wish this wasn't goodbye," Jo said, her eyes glistening.

"Then stick with me, kid." Wesley waved his fingers beside his mouth like he held an invisible cigar, then looped his arm through Jo's. "Ready to let me spend some of my ill-gotten gains on you?"

"Only if we go dutch," she insisted, making them all laugh. Dylan's smile lingered long after the shadowed dock obscured them from view.

Yes. He'd miss them.

Nolee most of all.

Her maturity in making the tough call to pull up stakes impressed the hell out of him. She'd grown from the reckless young woman he'd left in Kodiak to a wise and now seasoned captain. There weren't many people he'd trust more than Nolee to do what needed to be done out there at sea.

Would she be that careful with his heart if he entrusted it to her again?

He was running out of reasons to believe the answer would be no.

She was competent, focused, brave—everything.

Everything to him.

"Still here?"

He whirled at the soft voice behind him.

Nolee.

In the twilight, her skin glowed iridescent and smooth. Her eyes sparkled as bright as the growing starlight. And her lips. Suddenly he couldn't drag his eyes off their full shape. When her tongue darted out to lick her bottom lip, he nearly groaned out loud.

How he wanted her. Loved her, too, he realized.

But would it be enough?

For either of them?

Tomorrow, he reported back to base and resumed his military life. The old thrill of unknown adventures fizzled flat in his skull. For the first time in years, he wanted to plant himself in one spot. With one person.

Nolee.

He didn't want to let her go yet, damn it.

"I'm not ready for our time together to end," he said, settling his hands on her waist.

She went still and he found himself holding his breath, warring emotions erupting with what he wanted to hear and what he was afraid she would say.

"I'm not, either," she admitted finally, the lapels of her jacket parting as she lifted her hands to rest on his chest.

The clean scent of wildflowers drifted up from her skin, light and delicate. "In fact, I have some ideas…"

Thank You, God. Relief kicked through him with surprising force.

He caught her hand in his and nearly yanked her off her feet as he hustled her back to the now-empty pilothouse.

"So do I." His voice had deepened and grown rough, edgy with the primal, animalistic need she aroused in him.

Control, Holt, he ordered himself.

Tonight had to be memorable. Savored. One neither of them would ever forget.

She disappeared toward her stateroom while he grabbed the bottle of champagne he'd stashed in the fridge the last time they'd been in port, along with a couple of mismatched jelly glasses, then raced up the stairs two at a time.

He jerked to a halt at her doorway and blinked.

Nolee lounged on her bed. She'd shed her raingear and the white tank top and fitted jeans she wore revealed lush curves. Anticipation churned inside Dylan. The sight of her was enough to make a grown man weep in appreciation.

With her dark hair tumbling helter-skelter around her smooth shoulders, her glowing face makeup-free, her lips natural and full, she was beautiful and sexy without even trying. It did him in.

Then he looked into her eyes and his body hardened to instant attention at the heat simmering in their chocolate-brown depths. She didn't need to put much effort into seducing him—she could accomplish the task with a mere look. A lone touch. A single word. A fleeting smile.

Need, sharp and edgy, scraped through him, overwhelming him with the desire to yank her into his arms and spend the next several hours blocking out the last few stressful weeks, specifically the last few stressful hours. All he wanted to do was *drown* in her.

Control, Holt.

Get your bearings.

He forced himself to sit on the edge of the bed and peel the foil from the bottle top with shaking hands.

"What's that?"

She circled her arms around his neck and her breasts flattened against his back.

The cork popped in his hand and the fruity-sweet fizz tickled his nose. "A toast," he said in a hoarse voice, then poured the first glass.

She pressed light feathery kisses down one side of his neck and the fire inside him leaped higher. Hotter.

"What are we toasting?" she breathed in his ear before capturing the lobe and running her tongue along the sensitive shape.

His breathing quickened. Grew ragged. The sparkling wine trembled as he stood. He pulled her to her feet and passed her the glass. "Us. You. Me." He filled another cup then clinked it against hers.

"What does that mean?" she asked, her voice shaky. She stared at him over the rim of her cup as she sipped. The naked vulnerability of her unguarded expression, the hint of hope and trace of fear, seized his heart.

He bolted back his drink, then set it on the shelf behind him. Truth time.

"Since the moment I pulled you off the *Pacific Sun*, I haven't been able to stop thinking about you. I can't stop imagining how we might be together. God help me, but I won't let you go this time. I'm yours, Nolee. I don't know how the hell we're going to work this out, but I'm not walking away without you. Not running, no matter how hard this might get."

Her half-empty glass plunged from her fingers onto the floor in a cascade of drops. "I'm not letting you go, either."

"Damn right," he growled. Looking at her now, a powerful wave of tenderness flooded him. This woman meant everything to him. And he wanted, needed to show her that, make her understand how perfect they were for each other. How they absolutely, positively belonged to each other. He could make her happy. Fulfill her. He'd give her everything she'd ever had to do without in life and things she'd never even dreamed of.

"Nolee." Her name sounded like a hoarse rasp, filled with all the love and want and need she inspired. The instant their lips touched, he was lost.

His mouth melded with hers in a deep, hot, wet tongue-mating kiss that hinted at the act his body craved to share with her. Without breaking the kiss, he steered her backward a few steps to the bed. When her legs hit the mattress, he trailed his lips and tongue down her neck. God, the way she tasted…a heady combination of heat and spice that always left him hungry for more. Shaking with need.

He pulled her tank top over her head. She wasn't wearing a bra and the sight of her rounded breasts and hard, rosy nipples caused a growl to rumble in his throat.

His lips found hers again briefly before gliding over her delicate collarbone. His hands skimmed down to her jeans, which he quickly unfastened. Bending over her, he lashed at one peak with his tongue, unable to get enough of her, while his hands slipped beneath the waistband of her panties to cup the sweet curve of her ass. Her back arched as she pressed herself closer, unabashedly asking for more. An invitation he was more than ready to accept. He slid one arm around her waist, drawing her hips tight against his.

While his tongue laved her straining breasts, he pushed the denim and her panties over her hips. Licking a trail down the center of her torso, he lowered himself to his knees, bringing her jeans down with him. He helped her step out of her clothes, then looked up the curvy length of her gorgeous body and into her eyes, which glittered with arousal.

Reaching up, he teased her taut nipples, still damp from his mouth. She moaned and sank her fingernails into the tops of his shoulders, arching into his touch. Pressing his face against her belly, he traced the indent of her navel with his tongue. The musk of her arousal invaded his senses, making his head reel and his mouth water for a taste. His hands cruised to her hips and he urged her down until she perched on the edge of the bed, then ran one hand up her body and gently pressed her backward until she leaned on her elbows.

Grasping her knees, he spread her legs wide and avidly drank in the sight of her glistening sex. His blood surged in his groin. Barely holding on to his slipping control, he slid his hands beneath her, tugged her closer and settled her thighs over his shoulders before dragging his fingers over her warm cleft.

"Dylan," she gasped, her voice breaking on a ragged breath as he leaned forward and gave her folds a long, lazy lick. She was so damn hot. So very responsive.

Her feminine sigh deepened into a groan when he slipped two fingers inside her and slowly pumped while his lips and tongue pleasured her, licking, teasing, sucking, flicking, swirling.

His other hand skated up to her breasts and he teased her peaked nipples, rolling them between his fingers. She lifted writhing hips against him, seeking more, her breaths quickening into erratic puffs. He felt her body tense, her arousal tightening, until with a sharp cry she convulsed. With tremors shuddering through her, he slipped a third finger into her wet heat and drew her clitoris into his mouth. She gasped and arched her back as she screamed again.

This time, when the tremors subsided, he kissed his way up her body, then shifted her higher on the mattress. When he rose to his knees, she joined him.

"Let me," she whispered, raking off his shirt before unfastening his jeans and whisking them off.

"I'm not fighting you on that," he groaned. Dark need slithered through him as she unfurled a condom over his heavy erection.

With his gaze locked on hers, he lowered her back to the bed, settling himself between her splayed thighs. He brushed his erection along her silky, wet folds, then entered her in one long, deep stroke. The heat of her body clamped around him and sweat popped along his brow.

He held himself there a moment, feeling their hearts beat in sync, inside and out. The sound mesmerized him as it reverberated through him.

He watched her, unblinking, as they connected on a level they hadn't breached yet...ever. This wasn't a frenzy of sex to ease a wild craving. This was something deeper and more powerful. A joining.

He gritted his teeth against the intense pleasure and withdrew nearly all the way from her body. Dark lashes fanned against her scarlet cheeks and air rushed between her parted lips.

"Open your eyes." He whispered the ragged words through the heated inches between them, winning the attention of her passion-clouded gaze. He wanted to watch her eyes glaze over with pleasure, wanted her to see... really see that it was him, and only him, who could make her shatter.

Then he plunged again, deep, grinding his hips slowly

against hers. He shuddered at the sensation of sinking into her tight wet sheath, then withdrawing, again and again, the erotically slick friction jolting pleasure into his every nerve ending.

She bit the edge of his bottom lip, sucking it into her mouth before soothing the ache with her tongue. Meeting him thrust for thrust, she lifted her hips to take more of him. All of him.

His thrusts quickened, deepened, each one propelling him closer to the edge. Nolee's nails grazed his back and her breathy moans filled his ears. She wrapped her legs around his waist, urging him deeper, countering each thrust, her fingers digging into his tense shoulders.

They stayed that way, both straining for the unbelievable edge, pumping, pulling, chasing each other closer.

With a keening cry of satisfaction, Nolee dropped her head against the pillows, her dark hair ballooning into a soft, disheveled cloud around her beautiful face.

The orgasm ripped through her body—he could feel it, see it, practically taste the sweetness of it on his tongue. He enjoyed watching her shudder with the sensations, enjoyed knowing he was the source of her pleasure.

He knew he could make her happy.

This was just the start of it.

The muscles of her inner walls contracted around his sex in the most delicious way possible. Only when she'd finally stilled beneath him did he let himself go, burying his face in the soft curve of her neck and pouring himself into her, each hot pulse of pleasure ripping a harsh breath from his throat.

When his heart rate returned to something resembling normal, he kissed the soft skin behind her ear, then lifted his head. She slowly blinked, and he looked into the most beautiful eyes he knew he'd ever see.

"Hello," he said, running one hand up her torso to palm her breast and brush his thumb over the velvety tip.

"Oh," she gasped, breathy, shooting him a mock surprised look. "Are you still here?"

"Yep. You're stuck with me." He smiled into her shining eyes.

"Good," she sighed and angled up to brush his jaw with a feathery kiss before dropping down again, her heavy-lidded eyes fluttering, her lips curving into a smile. "I don't ever want to be apart."

"We won't be." Because they would find a way to make this work. They cared about each other too much not to.

When he took her out tomorrow, he'd do everything he could to convince her to leave Kodiak with him and start over. He rolled onto his side and gathered her in his arms, drifting toward sleep.

He'd keep her safe. She wouldn't spend another moment of her life feeling like she needed to prove anything.

Dylan would make sure of it.

15

NINE HOURS AND two condom wrappers later, Nolee twisted beneath the shower's pelting warm water, her muscles sore, her skin deliciously tender and raw. She rinsed the shampoo from her hair. The coconut scent revived her, despite the scant sleep she'd gotten after marathon sex with Dylan.

What an incredible night.

Fire fanned in her belly as she recalled Dylan's scorching touch. No one had ever brought her such exquisite satisfaction, such mind-blowing release, the way he did. For those hours, he'd tantalized and tormented her until she'd forgotten her anguish over her dreaded meeting with her Dunham Seafoods bosses tomorrow. Instead, she'd simply existed on a cloud of physical and emotional bliss.

Her heart swelled as she recalled Dylan's pledge to work things out and stay together. Once she convinced her employers to keep her on as captain, she'd have everything she ever wanted. Career and a committed relationship. Independence and love.

Could she have it all?

She grabbed a loofah sponge and squeezed bodywash onto it. It seemed too good to be true, but Dylan had helped her realize that she needed to stop questioning herself. She wouldn't give in to self-doubt again. Her father's abandonment didn't define her. In fact, now that she looked at it more closely, in some ways, his rejection had made her stronger, a woman who no longer chased after accolades and approval from strangers. A strong, independent woman who was capable of accomplishing anything she set her mind to achieving.

It was as if Dylan had flipped the lens through which she viewed herself. The new filter gave her a deeper perspective and peace with her life and, now, her future with Dylan.

A large, male body slipped into the tiled cubicle and turned her in the small space, breaking her from her thoughts.

"Dylan!"

He swooped down and captured her lips in a heart-melting kiss before pulling back, his handsome mouth curved in a sexy smile. Her body shivered and tensed as it remembered his, responding to him on contact.

"Morning, beautiful," he rumbled, his voice deep and rough, as he brushed back a wet lock of her hair. Spraying water plastered his curls to his head and his eyes darkened to the color of a deep pine forest beneath his long, spiked lashes.

"Morning," she breathed, feeling slightly dizzy with so much hard muscle all around her. She ate him up with her eyes. Droplets sluiced down his skin, finding secret paths along the hard ridges she ached to touch, to trace with her tongue.

His abs tightened as she skimmed her fingertips along the muscled crests and valleys, tracing the water-slick, chiseled six-pack of his torso and the ropy lengths of muscle in his arms. Her mouth watered as her eyes roved over him, heat flaring between her thighs at the way his pelvic muscles cut down in a sharp V that framed his long, thick arousal.

"Let me," he whispered in her ear, his voice gravelly with the same need that gripped her. Dylan plucked the loofah from her hand and her heart pounded a fervent acquiescence to his potent demand.

He slid the rough sponge over her stomach in lazy circles that set her skin ablaze. She groaned at the teasing, sensual brushes against her quivering flesh.

"Tell me how much you like this." His lips moved beside her ear, her body tightening in response to his whispered words. His ardent gaze made her feel beautiful.

"Don't stop," she panted then arched, thrusting her breasts against his sensually exploring hands as he whisked the sudsy pad up and across her aching peaks, rubbing gently, driving her wild. The hard length of his cock pressed against her stomach and she savored the feel of dark desire that wound together with the deep joy Dylan alone could give her.

She wanted him with a need that left her breathless, and yet the wanting was almost as delicious as knowing she'd have him. Soon. That state of delayed fulfillment stirred a hot tension inside her, a pleasurable ache.

Better still, she'd never have to stop wanting him because today was the first day of the rest of their lives together. Dylan had vowed that they'd make things work and she believed him with every bit of her heart. Trusted him completely. Her days of expecting disappointment, of guarding herself against vulnerability were over. With nothing left to fear, she could fully surrender her heart to the man who'd held it all along.

Dylan.

"So you like that?" he teased, his light tone at odds with the achingly serious, tender light in his eyes. His hand shook lightly and it moved her to see how she affected him. They'd crossed into deeper emotional waters and there was no going back.

"Yes. Oh, yes," she whimpered, needing him to cease his wicked torment, the tension building inside making her squirm. Her body trembled as she lifted herself on her toes to fit her curves to his hard flesh for one long, drawn-out moment, a backbone-melting experience.

Dylan's jaw turned to granite. His eyes flared, pupils dilated as he dropped the sponge and claimed her mouth again. His hot lips skated over hers, more demanding now than they'd been moments before, as droplets rained all around them.

Tongues dueled, lips sucked and short breaths wound together. The growling noise he made in his throat reverberated through the kiss as his tongue stroked over hers and their wet bodies slid over one another. Her elbow banged against the faucet as he pivoted her to the opposite wall. His bent head brushed against the shower dome.

None of it mattered.

At the delicious press of him against her, the crush of hard muscle against willing flesh, shivers chased each other up and down her spine. Her knees wobbled, leaving her no choice but to wrap her arms around his neck and hold on tight. He fingered a taut nipple. Her fingers explored the curls at the base of his scalp.

He tweaked the crest between his thumb and forefinger at the same time he nipped her lower lip and she practically convulsed with the sharp contraction of her feminine muscles.

She lifted one leg high alongside his, her knee parallel to his waist in a gesture that opened her to his straining erection. Heat burned in her, scorched through her veins, her limbs, her core.

And still his toe-curling kiss went on. She clutched at his shoulders, silently begging for him to join himself to her…the part of herself she now knew had been missing all along. Without him, she would never again feel complete.

"Condom. Sink."

It took her a moment to process the gasped words while he bent to kiss his way down her neck and into the V of her cleavage. He circled one nipple with his tongue while she reached outside the pounding water to find the foil packet he'd thoughtfully remembered to bring with him.

Jackpot.

She tore a strip of foil from the top of the wrapper and freed the condom. Her heart hammered in her chest, her erratic pulse a result of her smoldering hunger for Dylan and for all the things he could do to her.

He released her breast to look her in the eye for one passionate second, his emotion-filled gaze raking over her with intensity. In its depths, she glimpsed the same raw feeling that gripped her, a thrilling, gleeful, shout-at-the-top-of-your-lungs recognition that everything she felt, he felt, too.

She loved him and he loved her.

Words would come later. For now, they spoke with their hands. Their lips. Their bodies.

His cock was smooth and hot to touch as she eased the condom over his ridged length with some difficulty, since the head of him bobbed and strained closer to her thighs. When she had him fully sheathed, he kissed her again, covering her lips with his the way she wanted him to cover the rest of her.

She teased his outer thigh with a shift of her leg against his and he answered by raising her leg higher. The move made her very aware of her vulnerability to him, the knowledge sending a fresh twinge between her legs.

She wanted him so badly she writhed against him, desperate for the feel of his cock against her. He trapped her hands in his against the shower wall, holding her perfectly still as he kissed her. Only then did he allow the tip of him to brush her clit. That small contact incited a strangled cry in her throat, a mewling yelp that bore no resemblance to her speaking voice.

If she'd had her hands free, she would have used them to help guide him inside her, but instead he kissed and teased her, tormenting them both with glancing touches that built mutual anticipation to a perilous level. Nolee's whole body shook, her every breath focused on the exquisite pleasure of almost-touches that never gave her the full measure of the man she wanted.

The man she loved.

The scent of skin and sex and ocean permeated the fogging shower while the pelting water muffled the sounds of their quickening breaths. She longed and wanted, hungered and cried out for him, until finally he released her hands to take hold of her legs. He fit them both around his waist, holding her up with his strength and the leverage of the shower. Stretching his hands across her upper thighs, he opened her wider, splaying her sex to his erection for a pulse-pounding moment before he positioned himself to enter her.

She tilted her hips to receive him, trusting him to hold on to her even if she didn't make it easy. Never before had she felt this exposed, this vulnerable, this ready to open herself up, body, heart and soul, to a man she knew would never let her down.

Beneath her, Dylan whispered her name. He angled and bent his body against hers to fine-tune the thrust, stretching her. She reveled in the near discomfort of his size. No one else made her feel so much.

Physically and emotionally. He cupped her butt cheeks in his hands, shifting his position while he held her steady. Her breasts flattened against his chest, her slick body curving and softening to accommodate his hard angles and masculine strength.

His thrusts grew deeper and harder in the steam-filled shower. The sounds of their lovemaking—the touch of skin on skin, the tender words and soft encouragements—filled her ears.

Tension built inside her, the slow windup to a climax still taking her by surprise though he'd delivered that same powerful jolt to her body the night before. Dylan knew her better than she knew herself. He understood what she needed, gave more than what she would have imagined asking.

She clawed at his shoulders, needing to anchor herself before the bottom fell out of her world. Finding some purchase in his biceps, she held on as pleasure rushed at her and then over her, shattering her with such brutal efficiency that she collapsed against him, bucking and shaking with the force of her fulfillment. She covered his face with kisses and cries of completion, the bliss so enormous, she had to share it.

Dylan's body froze the next moment, a paralyzed second as he found his own fulfillment, while her reward went on and on. Dylan's guttural shout mingled with her screams as Nolee slumped in the circle of his arms, unable to think or move or speak for the next few minutes. She barely managed to breathe in and breathe out, the rhythmic motion and jetting shower eventually forcing her heart rate to slow.

And even after the shudders ceased and their breathing quieted, they remained there, lulled by each other's heartbeats. When full awareness returned, she peeled herself off the shower wall while Dylan straightened, flicked off the tap, then wrapped her carefully in a towel, the tender gesture touching her. Surely he must love her the way she loved him.

She couldn't wait to tell him. Couldn't wait to hear him say it back. Once she had convinced her bosses to keep her on as captain, she hoped to begin her new life, Dylan by her side.

Several hours later, Nolee sat across from Dylan in the very restaurant he'd taken her to the night of their prom. Little had changed, she mused, taking in the elegant table linens and crystal glasses, the strong feel of his fingers twined with hers, the tender, loving expression on his face.

Only now they'd matured. Had had life experiences apart from one another that'd led them right back to this moment…this second chance.

"What are you thinking?" he asked, turning her hands in his, rubbing his thumbs across her palms.

"How happy I am."

His warm eyes crinkled at her. "Me, too. And I've got news I hope will make us both even happier."

"You do?" She blinked at him a moment, processing.

"The Coast Guard air station we'll be transferred to. My commander phoned this morning. One of their rescue swimmers is getting promoted and they have an opening if I want it."

Throat dry, she lifted her water glass and downed a quick gulp. Her heart thudded loudly in her ears. "*We'll* be transferred?"

He leaned forward and squeezed her numb fingers. "That was a crass way to say it. I'm sorry, Nolee. What I meant is, will you come to Cape Cod with me?"

Dismay rose, wet and cold, a dark arctic tide that froze her heart solid. She yanked her hands from his. Clasped them, twisting, on her lap as she trembled at the sudden chasm-opening revelation.

"You're still transferring? I thought…since you hadn't mentioned it in so long…"

Dylan's eyebrows crowded each other over the bridge of his nose. "There was a delay in approval because my commander had to complete an audit. Plus, since this is an out-of-rotation-year assignment request, we had to wait until a spot opened up."

She sat very still, as if somehow she could turn herself to stone. Not feel any of this. "So, you just thought I'd go with you?" she asked through numb, stiff lips.

He stared at her, unblinking for a moment, then shook his head. "I thought, after last night…" He cleared his throat. Began again. "We talked about it…"

She raised a shaking finger. Pointed. "You said you wouldn't leave me. That we'd work things out."

Betrayal forked inside her. Flash-white lightning in a black sky.

"I'm not, and we will. I'm taking you with me." He released a quick breath. "I mean, we're going together. I hope," he ended, belatedly.

Somewhere in the room a group began singing a discordant, joyful rendition of the Happy Birthday song.

"No. We're not."

The color drained from Dylan's face. "But I thought you'd want to leave, since you didn't make your quota."

"What does that have to do with anything?"

He stared at her, stunned. Silence sliced the air between them. When he began again, his words emerged slowly, halting, as if they had a bad taste.

"You needed to reach your numbers for Dunham Sea-foods to keep you on and the chances of another offer aren't great. You're an incredible captain, but this is a tough business, especially at your age, and after losing a boat…"

Each word stabbed straight through her, as if puncturing a lung. She struggled to drag in air. Her chest burned, afire. Raucous applause rose from the partying group and forks clanged on glasses.

Once the noise quieted, she countered, "I don't know that. Not until I talk to my bosses. Do you think I'd quit without trying?"

"It's not giving up…it's being realistic. In Cape Cod, you can start over. Get a small boat and be your own captain. Fish for lobster or stay home. No matter what, I'll take care of you. Make you happy. Keep you safe," he insisted, his eyes earnest. Concerned. Sincere.

And clueless.

"Do you think I care about being 'safe'? That I want to be taken care of? Made happy?" She held her tongue until the partying group stopped chanting about presents, then continued. "I can do those things on my own, Dylan. I just want you in my life. Here."

"I won't stay in Kodiak. You know that." Across the table, he watched her with electric intensity.

"Why? Why would I know that?" Her insides felt like ground meat. Pulverized. Raw. "You've been happy in Alaska. Admit it. I saw you on the boat."

"It's not enough. There's too many bad memories here. Come with me," he implored. His jittering knee hit the underside of the table. "We'll make new memories. Wonderful ones. You won't miss Kodiak. Not much. Promise."

"You don't know me," she whispered, more to herself then him. Her index finger swept a clear line in the condensation beading on her water glass.

"Yes I do, Nolee." He stared down at the table for a moment, then looked up at her. "No one knows you better.

You don't always know when to cut your losses—this is one of those times."

Their waitress appeared, dropped the check onto the table and retreated, her smile fading as her head swiveled between them.

"I don't cut and run, Dylan. That's you." Her voice came out harder than she'd wanted and she swallowed, struggling to ignore her bone-crushing pain. "Do you ever see yourself settling down in one place? Being happy with the same thing day after day?"

Shock and hurt darkened his eyes. He angled back in his chair as if she'd struck him. "No. But I want you in my life. That's big for me, Nolee."

"It's not enough." She dropped her head into her palm and took a deep breath. "I need roots, and you want to wander."

"You've always been a risk-taker. Fearless." She felt his fingers brush hers and she pulled back as if stung. "Yet you're scared to take a chance on me. On us."

She lifted her head, opened her mouth to deny the accusation then shut it. A world of experience, her entire vagabond childhood, had taught her to be cautious. "I won't give up my entire life the way my…the way my mother did."

He shook his head slowly after a brief silence. "I'm not like your father."

Outside, the sun appeared through a cloud and beamed a shaft of angled light directly at their table. Nolee blinked stinging eyes in the sudden brightness.

"Yes. You are," she said, fierce. "He couldn't settle down. What happens when you get tired of me? Or leave when we have problems? I'd have sacrificed my life to be a part of yours and be left with nothing…nothing of my own…just like my mom."

"I won't ever get tired of you," Dylan insisted, his voice cracking, splintering, his expression shattered. "I'd never abandon you."

"Wouldn't you? You left your parents without saying goodbye. Haven't even attempted to keep in touch."

His jaw turned to granite. "That's not the same thing. Not even close."

"Your family is the part of Kodiak you can't deal with."

"Maybe once. But not anymore. I stopped caring about them a long time ago."

He really didn't get it. How wrong she'd been to hope this time together would be different.

"You don't know anything, Dylan Holt. And you won't stay in one place long enough to figure anything out— including yourself. What's that line from that old movie we used to like? The one with the shrimp boat captain…?"

He raised an eyebrow. "Forrest Gump?"

A thunderous crash of breaking china and glass erupted from the kitchen, silencing them momentarily. A couple of hustling waitresses whisked by.

"That's it. Remember when Forrest's mother said, 'You've got to put the past behind you before you can move on.'"

He nodded.

"We can't have a future until you've settled things with them."

"They have nothing to do with us, Nolee."

"Yes they do. They made mistakes, and someday, I might, too. But people who care about each other stick around. Try to work things out. I understand that you were hurt as a kid. But now you have a chance to make things right. Are you going to see them before you leave?"

"No." He ran a hand through his curls and shifted in his seat. "There's nothing there for me anymore."

She let out a long breath and stood. Her hands gripped the back of her chair as she waited for her wobbling knees to steady.

"There's nothing here with me, either," she said over the painful tightness of her throat. "I'm sorry."

"Nolee!" He caught her hand. "Stay."

She battled the magnetic pull that threatened to sweep her off her feet and carry her straight to Dylan. The familiar scent of him flooded her senses with a longing so fierce it was a physical ache. If only she could dial back the clock and rush into his arms one last time. "That's what I'm asking you to do, but you won't…will you?"

Stay with me, she added silently, studying the ceiling, willing away the wet rushing to her eyes.

Want me.

Try for me.

There was another silence. She felt the hurt in it, and was crushed.

After a charged moment, she forced herself to keep speaking when all she wanted to do was cry and cry and cry.

"Please see them, at least. If not for my sake, then your own. Goodbye."

"I'M PROUD OF YOU, Nolee. You leaned in when you could have given up and now look at you."

Aunt Dai beamed across her kitchen island at Nolee a week later. Her knife slashed through a head of garlic, a flashing silver blur. Behind her, oil popped in a cast-iron skillet atop her gas stove.

"You're a captain for some big shot *gussuks*," she crowed, using their slang for non-Inuits. She brandished her knife. "Lots of money."

At a loud snort across the room, Nolee looked up. Her

mother, Kathy, wheeled her oxygen tank to a small bay window. Outside, icicles dripped from eaves and melting snow slid from two snowmobiles parked in front of her relative's small wood cabin. A midday sun burned through a gap in the fat-bellied clouds blotting out the sky.

"Thanks, Aunt Dai." Nolee mustered up a half smile that fell almost immediately.

"Money is not happiness," her judgmental parent pronounced.

True enough, she thought, given her complete and total misery.

When she'd walked away from Dylan, a part of her had ripped loose and stayed behind, leaving her empty. Hollow. And in that vacuum, she'd caved in on herself, a black hole replacing her heart, the spaces inside her growing denser and heavier by the minute.

Had he left Kodiak yet?

By now, he could have signed his papers and transferred thousands of miles away. The painful thought wrapped around her heart like barbed wire.

It was exactly what he wanted.

And she had exactly what she wanted, too, she reminded herself firmly. Dunham Seafoods had surprised her by offering her another one-year contract. While she'd fallen short of her quota, she'd still done enough in terms of safety and catch to convince them to rehire her. She'd achieved every last bit of independence she'd craved, yet she'd hardly slept or eaten since parting with Dylan.

On a mat by the door, her aunt Dai's husky whined in her sleep, her legs paddling in some unseen chase. Nolee wished she could run from her tortured thoughts, too. Her second-guessing.

Why wasn't she happy about her career coup, at least? She twisted the apple she was peeling for tonight's cobbler and caught her mother's frown. *The hollows in her cheeks look deeper today*, Nolee observed, her ever-present worry for her parent rising higher than ever.

"What will you do with all that money?" Aunt Dai angled her knife and began chopping in the opposite direction.

Nolee continued skimming her paring knife around her apple. "I'm going to put down a deposit on a house for Mom and me."

"Keep it." Her mother untangled her oxygen tank's tube and lowered herself into a rocking chair. "I want no part of that money."

Nolee winced. No matter how hard she tried, she'd never, ever be good enough for her mother. Still, she wouldn't quit on her family. Dylan might be able to turn his back on loved ones, but not her. One of the many reasons they weren't right for each other.

So why couldn't she stop missing him? The ache of it throbbed so hard she had to bite the inside of her cheek to contain herself.

With a flick of her wrist, Aunt Dai tossed the garlic in the pan where it splattered and hissed. The savory, pungent smell wove through the toasty kitchen. "Ah, Kathy. Get with the times. Stop being so old-fashioned."

"The old ways are good."

A buzzing microwave dinged and Aunt Dai pulled the door open and spoke over her shoulder. "What can I say, Nolee? Your mother is stubborn."

"So am I." Nolee mindlessly swept her knife around her last apple, the peel curling over her fingers in one long piece. "Don't you want to settle down, Mother?"

The diabetic monitor on her hip beeped, and Nolee eyed the pump's red light. Concern rose. "Blood sugar's low."

She yanked open the fridge, poured a glass of orange juice and hustled to her mother's side. "Here. Drink."

Kathy's slim, elegant fingers wrapped around the glass and tipped it up to her mouth. After a long gulp, Nolee stayed her attempt to put it back down. "All of it, please."

With a sigh, her mother drained it down to the last drop. "I don't want you hovering over me."

"I'm not!" Nolee cried as she bent over her pale parent. She caught her aunt's arched brow and dropped into a seat. "Okay. Maybe. But I worry about you. I want you to have the best of everything."

Her mother shrugged and plucked a roasted nut from a nearby bowl. "I already have that."

"You don't have a place to call your own."

A pulverized shell disintegrated between the metal arms of a cracker. "I have what I need. That's all I want."

Somewhere, a phone shrilled, and Aunt Dai hustled out of the room to grab it.

Nolee watched her mother chewing a walnut, her expression far away.

"Don't you want your independence? You'd never have to ask anyone for help. You'd never feel like less than others."

Her mother's eyes swerved to Nolee. Narrowed. "Less than? You think I feel like I'm not as good as other people?"

Nolee ducked her head. "You don't have anything. I mean, we didn't."

"We had—*have* plenty. Here." She tapped her chest. "You think money—things—they make you better? A stronger person? No. They make you weak. You become a slave to them, always wanting more, never satisfied. Gifts make slaves as whips make dogs."

"That's not true," Nolee insisted. "Dad left us with nothing. We struggled."

Her mother reached out and smoothed back a lock of Nolee's hair. "He left me with everything I could ever want." Her eyes searched her daughter's. "You."

Nolee blinked fast at the sudden, stinging rush of tears. "But I wasn't enough."

"Of course you were. Your father…" Her mother swatted the air with her hand. "He's the one who's had to do without. Without you. I pity him."

"And I hate him," Nolee declared, the bitter words dredged from a dark, hollow place.

Her mother covered her hands with hers. "Seek strength," her mother quoted. "Not to be greater than my brother, but to fight my greatest enemy, Myself."

Nolee froze. "What do you mean?"

Kathy stared at her wordlessly for a long moment.

"So I'm my own enemy?" Nolee demanded.

At the continued lack of response, she bolted to her feet and paced. The husky's tail thumped against the wood floor as she approached, then stilled when she pivoted and trod away.

"I don't hate myself."

More silence.

"I—I— Oh, Mom." Nolee sank back into her chair and covered her face. Her shoulders shook as she wept because she did, she saw it now. She did think she wasn't worthy. Why else had she worked so hard to prove herself? Not to anyone else. Not to her mother. No. Not even to her father.

She'd wanted to prove her worth to herself, she realized, her harshest critic of all.

A warm arm settled around her shoulders. Squeezed. "You have a right to happiness."

Nolee swiped her damp cheeks and blinked up at her

mother, her strong, independent parent, who'd never had to depend on anyone else for happiness, for love, because she'd determined the form those took for herself.

Should Nolee?

Suddenly she understood the real reason she'd pushed Dylan away. It was insecurity. Not independence. Fear instead of love.

She shoved herself to her feet and swept her mother into a bear hug. "I love you, Mom. Tell Aunt Dai not to set a place for me at dinner."

"Where are you going?"

Nolee grabbed her keys and jacket and stopped at the door. "To get my head on straight."

And her heart.

Was it too late for her and Dylan?

16

DYLAN STOMPED ON his parents' icy stoop and eyed the doorbell. Funny how it looked lower than he remembered. The door smaller. Even the house astonished him. He eyed the snow-laden roof beneath heavy clouds. Noted the stainless steel pipe belching cedarwood smoke. Once he'd thought this black paper and particleboard house luxurious.

A paradise…a refuge.

Especially those times he'd stumbled toward it out of the dark, hungry-thirsty-cold after his father dragged them on wilderness challenges in rugged backcountry. It'd been one of the survivalist exercises comprising his exacting "commando" upbringing. The kind that'd turn them into real men, his father vowed.

Anger flared in his gut. Shot up in his esophagus and burned.

What the hell was he doing here after all these years?

Nolee.

His jaw clenched so hard his back teeth ached. He forced his balled hands to unfurl. A brisk wind rattled around the house's northern corner. Glittering snow particles, as fine as crushed glass, showered him.

She'd challenged him to face his past. Claimed he'd

never put it behind him otherwise. Insisted they couldn't be together until he did.

All week, he'd thrown himself into his work, flying back-to-back missions, training staff, working out every free moment of the day until his body collapsed. Anything to keep his mind off Nolee. None of it worked.

Out of the corner of his eye, a deer and her offspring glided out of the woods then froze at the sight of him. He held his breath until they pivoted and leaped away. Their white tails bobbed once in the gloom then vanished, the trampled snow the only evidence he hadn't imagined them.

Life was like walking through snow.

Every step showed.

What had his time here in Kodiak revealed?

That he still loved Nolee.

No matter how far he traveled, he'd never leave his feelings for her behind.

Sometimes he caught himself staring at her contact number in his phone. He imagined her voice, her smile, the light in her eyes when she'd teased him. He thought about her hot, eager body beneath his, and the way her touch set him on fire and then healed him a moment later, the scars of his childhood smoothing and becoming a badge of honor instead of his secret shame.

His final conversation with Nolee ran through his brain on a permanent loop. Her wounded face was always with him.

The thing that plagued him, that left him sleepless and numb, was the way they'd left things. He hadn't even said goodbye.

Damn it. He shoved his hands in his pockets. He needed to compartmentalize. Leave her and his family behind in Kodiak and get on with the rest of his life, no matter how empty the road ahead appeared.

He pictured the unsigned rotation paperwork beside his bunk. When he got back to base, he'd quit stalling and turn it in. Once this family visit ended, Kodiak and his past would finally release him for good.

Taking a deep breath, he pressed the doorbell. Waited. Pressed again. His heart pounded in his ears.

The door lurched open and his mother froze in the entryway. Her hand fluttered to the small, heart-shaped locket he'd gotten her one Mother's Day. "Dylan!"

"May I come in?"

"Of course! Come in. Come in." She jerked back and retreated a couple of paces. "You should have told me you were coming; I would have made a roast."

"I can't stay long." Uneasy, he slid inside and shut the door behind him. In a flash, he was sixteen again, then twelve, eight.

Out of ingrained habit, he stepped out of his boots, hung up his coat and followed her past a closed pocket door that now sealed off the living room archway.

His mother reached for a mug hanging above the stove. "Let me make you coffee."

"No need to fuss."

"Then what can I get you? Soda?" His mother's movements looked jerky as she set down the cup, her eyes jumping from place to place, red blotches blooming on her neck. He perched on one of the kitchen's backless stools and drummed his fingers on his knees.

This was all a mistake.

He shouldn't have come.

She opened the fridge and spoke over her shoulder. "I just fixed a nice ham sandwich for your father. I'll make you one."

His stomach tightened at the mention of his oppressive

parent. "Please don't bother. I just wanted to let you know I'm leaving Kodiak soon."

"Well look what the cat dragged in," boomed a voice behind Dylan. "Ma said she invited you over."

He twisted around, rose and automatically grabbed the hand thrust at him.

"Didn't actually think you'd come." Robbie arched an eyebrow.

"Me, neither." Bemused, he stared down at his big brother, a vantage point he'd never had growing up. Odd.

"What are they feeding you in the Coast Guard? Shit. Ma, how tall do you think Dyl is?" Robbie stuck his hand in an open bag of chips, then deposited one in his mouth. Chewed.

She angled a knife over a sandwich and cut it in the precise, diagonal direction Dylan's father preferred. "Well over six feet, I'd say."

Robbie leaned a hip against the countertop. "I'm five ten and you've got me beat by five inches. No more whupping your ass in the wrestling ring."

"Four," Dylan corrected, feeling his shoulders begin to loosen, lower. Robbie? Admitting Dylan could ever best him in anything?

"Whatever, asshole. Hey. Wanna ride with me up to Bear Trap Lake and go ice fishing? If you still remember how…"

Dylan closed his mouth around the quick *yes* that rushed up and over his tongue. A longing to hang out at the spot where they'd held their annual fishing derbies seized him. His dad had turned it into a nail-biting, stomach-cramping competition for who caught the biggest and most trout. But there had been good moments, too…

"Nah. I'm heading out in a few minutes. Just wanted to stop in like I said I would, and now that I have, I'll be—"

His brother squared off against him. "You'll be what? Running away? Again?"

"I'm not running away," he denied, his mind returning to Nolee. "I'm here, aren't I?"

"Yeah. For two seconds."

A beeper rang from the counter beside his mother and she jumped.

"What's that?" Dylan asked.

"Dad." A cloud seemed to pass over Robbie's face.

Dylan's muscles clenched. "He can't even come in for his own sandwich?"

Leave it to his father to interrupt even this small reconciliation. Not that he wanted to see the jerk. But he didn't have to make everyone jump to do his bidding every second of every day.

"No. Honey. It's just—"

The beeper buzzed again. Louder. Harder. Longer. Short, staccato beats. Demanding. He could hear his father's voice in it.

Dylan snatched up the plate. "I'll take it to him."

"No. Dylan. Wait!"

He ignored their protests and marched into the living room, his mother following close behind.

The sight of a wheelchair pulled him up short. A small, old man slumped in it, his chin resting on his concave chest.

Sharp dark eyes swerved to him. Narrowed.

The plate dropped to the floor. Shattered.

"Dad?"

His mom's trembling hand fell on Dylan's arm. Squeezed. "I wanted to tell you at the restaurant, but your father insisted he didn't want a pity visit from you."

"The hell he'd get one," Dylan declared. The room seemed to tilt slightly.

"Damn straight," barked his father in the gruff voice of his childhood. It rammed straight down through Dylan's vertebrae, locking each one. "Have a seat, son."

He gestured to the couch beside him, as in command as ever, then wheeled himself to face it once Dylan and Robbie perched on its edge.

"What happened to—"

At his father's raised hand, Dylan snapped his mouth shut. Swallowed back his questions. Old habits die hard, he thought as he watched his broom-wielding mother whisk ceramic shards into a dustpan.

"Six months ago. Ischemic stroke. You were in that Saint Thomas hurricane. Your mother couldn't reach you. I told her not to bother when I woke." His jaw jutted. "You are not to blame your mother."

Regret, heavy and tight, banded around Dylan's chest. Oh. His proud, proud father.

He could have lost him.

"Yes, sir," Dylan exclaimed, mind racing. He should have known about this, damn it, but his father was right. His mother, who rarely went against her husband, wasn't completely responsible.

Dylan had played his part, too.

He'd turned his back on them. Walked away. Put distance between him and a complicated relationship…just like Nolee said.

"Sandwich, Marlene."

"Coming up, Joe." Dylan's mother disappeared into the kitchen.

"I'll take one, too—oomph!" Robbie's voice cut off when Dylan jabbed his side with his elbow.

He spied a scrapbook on a coffee table. "What's this?" He stood and flipped through it silently, then returned to the first page, which held a large picture of Dylan in his graduation gown. "Where'd you get this?"

"We took it." His mother returned, handed over a fresh sandwich to his dad then drew back when he waved away her efforts to tuck a napkin into his collar.

Surprise walloped the backs of Dylan's knees. "Huh? You were there?"

"You graduated with honors." His father nodded to himself as he chewed, then continued. "We were proud of you."

"Proud?" Dylan asked, skeptical. All he'd heard, all his life, was every which way he'd let down his old man, including, and especially, his lack of interest in the family excursion business.

He flipped through the pages again. Each one held articles and pictures chronicling his rescues and places he'd been stationed with the Coast Guard. "Why do you have these?"

"Pop here's obsessed." Robbie crossed his arms over his chest and rolled his eyes.

"Bullshit," Dylan bit out and met his father's stare head-on. "Sir." Here it was. Clear-cut evidence that he cared. Exactly what Dylan had chased after, dreamed about, despaired over getting as a boy. Nothing he'd done had ever made a damn difference then.

"Dylan. Please don't talk that way to your father."

He strode to the window and peered out at the gray day. His thoughts wrestled each other, piling on top of one another, struggling to free themselves.

"The boy's got a right, Marlene."

At his father's unexpected words, he whirled.

"Excuse me?"

"I said it." His father brushed a veined hand over his head. "I wasn't the best dad."

Robbie's snort cut off at their mother's death glare.

"Of course, you were a regular pain in the ass, too," continued his father. "Stubborn. Rebellious. Hotheaded. Always wanted to go your own way. Got that from me."

Dylan's mouth dropped open.

"When we sent you off to live with Bill, it didn't take me more than a week to regret it. But I was too proud to go after you. Figured you'd come around eventually. Sure as hell wasn't going to go crawling. Never thought you'd leave Kodiak for good, though."

His words punched Dylan in the gut. Air rushed out of him, leaving a sickening sensation in the pit of his stomach.

"Reading about all you've done in the Coast Guard, the people you've helped, the lives you've saved…well… it opened my eyes. I should have supported you instead of trying to hold you back. Because of that, I didn't just lose a guide for the business, I lost a son. I don't want to lose you again, if you'll give your old man another chance."

"No."

At Dylan's sharp word, his brother bolted to his feet and his mother gasped.

His father hung his head and spoke to his lap. "Well. Guess I deserve that."

Two strides closed the distance between them. Dylan dropped to one knee beside his dad. "NO. I mean that you're not taking all the blame. Jesus. It always has to be about you."

Silence. Then his father's sudden laugh rumbled from him, his brother's guffaws mingling. "Son of a—"

"I screwed up, too." Dylan crushed his eyes closed for a moment, willing the sting in them away. "I shouldn't have left Kodiak without a goodbye and I should have kept in touch. This separation's my fault, too. I—I'm sorry, Dad. Mom. Robbie."

"Ah. Don't get all soft on me, now," griped his dad as he returned Dylan's fierce hug.

"I hope you'll stay for dinner, sweetheart." His mother's vanilla scent enveloped him as she kissed the top of his head. "We need to make up for lost time before you transfer."

Dylan straightened, thinking fast. "Actually, I'm not so sure I'm leaving."

He'd not only pushed his family away for past hurts, he'd done the same to Nolee. He saw now that he had preferred distance from people. Had beaten a path away from them to have it. He couldn't do that with Nolee, too. Or himself.

He deserved love after all and had the right to home and hearth and family. Gone were his days of wandering. He wanted to stay in one spot, Nolee his North. His South. His East and West.

"I have to go. But I'll be back."

And he would. First stop would be to his commander's office to rescind his out-of-rotation-year transfer request. He wanted a life here with Nolee and his family. With three and a half years left for this regular rotation, and another three to four years if he requested a follow-on tour and an additional twelve-month extension, he'd have enough time to cement his relationship with his family...and start one of his own, he hoped, with his first and only love.

Nolee.

FROM THE *PACIFIC DAWN'S* BOW, Nolee watched the sunset bleed orange and blue into the edge of the earth. The sea, sparkling indigo, was benign and calm, and the deck hardly moved as the boat floated serenely in her slip. Silent gulls perched like stone sentries atop the pier's wooden poles. Some poked their bills beneath lifted wings while others sank onto their webbed feet, eyes closed.

She tipped her head back and her lungs expanded, drawing in a long cold gulp of salted air. Usually she relished solitary moments like this on deck, quiet times when the ship slumbered. The one time she could imagine herself the only person in the world. Except now, after these passion-filled weeks with Dylan, she no longer wanted to be alone, an island, a woman unto herself.

Her gaze swept one last time over these beloved waters, this ship, and she mentally said her goodbye. Kodiak had been her home, her refuge and comfort. But it wasn't her heart. That belonged to Dylan. Now that she'd made up her mind to leave and find him and had formally resigned from Dunham Seafoods after a quick meeting with her bosses, she suddenly couldn't wait to go.

At a light step behind her, she whirled.

"Dylan!"

He strode across the deck, tall, broad-shouldered and impossibly handsome in a hunter-green parka, jeans and work boots. Her heart stalled for a long moment, then picked up a high-speed thump like a coiler winching full blast. "What are you doing here?"

"I just saw my parents." He reached for her hand, enveloping her fingers in his.

"You did?" she asked, struggling, the act of communicating or thinking right now with him so close nearly impossible. "Then you know about your dad. I didn't want to keep it a secret, but your mother insisted your father should be the one to tell you…"

He tugged her closer, oblivious to the occasional fisherman wandering along the dock. "She was right. If I'd known, I might not have visited for the right reasons."

"Why did you go?"

"You," he rasped. His hands skimmed up her spine. "I couldn't stop thinking about what you said in the restaurant. About needing to face my past and reconcile it before moving on."

A sinking thought bowed her head. "So you came here as part of your goodbye?" She wanted to go with him, but what if he'd changed his mind and didn't want her anymore?

He gently touched her face. "No."

"No?" She lifted her chin.

"Those things you said about me being closed off? Distancing myself? All true. Or they were before, but I'm different now. You…this time together…it changed me. I want a family. A home. A future with you, Nolee. And I'm not leaving Kodiak. At least, not until I have to."

Everything went still as she processed what he'd said. He was staying here? Willing to give up the excitement of traveling the world? On the heels of her amazement, however, concern followed.

It'd be easy to agree and stay. This was the only world she knew, and she feared leaving it. She'd be ten kinds of a fool to say no to him, but she'd come too far to go back to the cautious woman she'd been. "No."

"No?" The light seemed to fade from his eyes, a lowering shade.

"I mean that you don't need to leave me. I want to go with you."

His arms tightened around her as he turned her away from an oncoming knot of fishermen. "You've got a career here that you've busted your tail to break into. How can you even think about walking away?"

"I can fish anywhere. Maybe I'll even buy my own boat." She liked the sound of that, liked the idea of being her own boss in a way that'd be even more autonomous than working for Dunham Seafoods. "It wouldn't be as big, but I'd call all the shots."

"And you'd do that just so I could transfer?" He didn't look skeptical so much as…astonished.

Men! If he was willing to make a few changes for her sake, then he should be able to accept that she would do the same for him. Then again, no one had ever put him first before. Certainly not his father, who'd dragged him through backcountry for most of his childhood, reprimanding him every step of the way for never proving himself to the family.

In that moment, Nolee felt the last remnants of her fear channel into a new, fierce protectiveness for Dylan. A desire to be there by his side, supporting him, loving him, in countless states. Countries even. Instead of making love in Alaska, they could lose their inhibitions on far-flung beaches and sultry seas.

The group of laughing fishermen passed on the pier, whistling and shouting for them to get a room. Nolee didn't care. Dylan didn't even register it. The man's ability to focus was awe-inspiring, especially when she happened to be at the center of all that intense attention.

Now to convince him she wanted this for both of them so he didn't pull some selfless hero crap and decide to plant himself in Kodiak anyway. She could, and would, be a captain anywhere, but there was only one Coast Guard and that meant traveling. "Being a rescue swimmer is all you ever wanted."

"You're what I want, Nolee." His green eyes were all on her and she felt his sincerity, down to her toes. "You make me happy."

"But Dylan," she argued, needing him to see that he didn't have to sacrifice after all. "I don't want you to—"

"God, woman," he cut in. Everything he was feeling was right there in his eyes—a hint of exasperation, a touch of laughter. "You are difficult."

"I'm not!" she insisted. "It's just that I—"

"You lock your jaw and won't let go, and I'm helpless." He cradled her face in his hands, stroked her cheek with one finger. Her knees almost buckled from the sweetness of the gesture.

"Every time, I'm completely helpless with you, Nolee. The way we fight is exhausting and hot and exhilarating and frankly weird. But you know what? I can't imagine sparring with anyone else."

He leaned closer, brushing the softest whisper of a kiss over her temple. "Kissing anyone else."

"Dylan," she murmured.

"Making love to anyone else." He slid his hand down to her hip and then spanned the circumference of her waist. "I'm glad you made me leave years ago. Otherwise, I'd never have anything to compare to the way I feel about you."

Tenderness and heat mingled in his eyes. Maybe even a little awe. "I'm in love with you."

Happiness bloomed inside and she sucked in a breath. It was like being winded. She grabbed hold of his shoulders. The declaration felt so solemn, so significant. "You're insane. You know that?"

One side of his mouth hitched up. "Yes. Yes, I do." Dylan swooped down and his lips captured hers. He kissed her with hunger and longing, his hands pressing her whole body to his in a head-to-toe connection.

Nolee broke the contact, not ready to lose herself in a sensual firestorm just yet. She had something important to say. Pulling back, she put her hands on his chest for a very temporary barrier.

"I love you, too." She blurted out the words with zero finesse and all feeling.

Dylan's face exploded in a smile and he gave her another teasing kiss, his palms covering her butt and pressing her against him right…

There.

She shivered in response. This definitely felt right. Clear down to her toes. "And sooner or later I have to leave Kodiak. No. I *need* to leave Kodiak. I want to see more of the world with you, travel together. How about we leave after your tour of duty in three years?"

He nodded, his eyes bright.

"I know there're plenty of beautiful places in the world," she added. "But you're the only home I need. I'll follow you anywhere."

"Anywhere?" He grinned that purely male smile that made her insides melt. The fierce heat assured her that he would be as passionate about keeping her near as he'd been, once, about keeping his distance.

"I might have one place in particular in mind." He swept an arm down behind her knees and tugged her off her feet.

A small squeal of surprise burst from her throat and she wound her arms around his neck as he crossed the deck to the wheelhouse. She snuggled against his broad chest, knowing exactly where he was headed, and more than ready to follow.

* * * * *

COMING NEXT MONTH FROM

HARLEQUIN *Blaze*

Available April 18, 2017

#939 UP IN FLAMES
by Kira Sinclair

Photographer Lola Whittaker didn't intend to rekindle the flames between her and sexy smoke jumper Erik McKnight—she just climbed into the wrong bunk. And now she's pregnant!

#940 PLAYING DIRTY
by Taryn Leigh Taylor

Hockey star Cooper Mead won't let anything stop him from finally leading the Portland Storm to championship victory...but sexy, smart-mouthed bartender Lainey Harper is turning into one hell of a distraction...

#941 TEMPTING KATE
Wild Wedding Nights • by Jennifer Snow

Wedding planner Kate Hartley needs a big win to save her business, so why is the groom's brother, sexy resort owner Scott Dillon, trying to stop the wedding of the century?

#942 BEYOND THE LIMITS
Space Cowboys • by Katherine Garbera

Going to space has been astronaut Antonio Curzon's dream forever, and nothing—not even oh-so-tempting teammate and competitor Isabelle Wolsten—will stand in his way.

YOU CAN FIND MORE INFORMATION ON UPCOMING HARLEQUIN® TITLES,
FREE EXCERPTS AND MORE AT WWW.HARLEQUIN.COM.

HBCNM0417

Get 2 Free Books,
Plus 2 Free Gifts—
just for trying the Reader Service!

 HARLEQUIN *Desire*

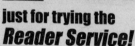

YES! Please send me 2 FREE Harlequin® Desire novels and my 2 FREE gifts (gifts are worth about $10 retail). After receiving them, if I don't wish to receive any more books, I can return the shipping statement marked "cancel." If I don't cancel, I will receive 6 brand-new novels every month and be billed just $4.80 per book in the U.S. or $5.49 per book in Canada. That's a savings of at least 8% off the cover price! It's quite a bargain! Shipping and handling is just 50¢ per book in the U.S. and 75¢ per book in Canada.* I understand that accepting the 2 free books and gifts places me under no obligation to buy anything. I can always return a shipment and cancel at any time. Even if I never buy another book, the 2 free books and gifts are mine to keep forever.

225/326 HDN GLPZ

Name _____ (PLEASE PRINT)

Address _____ Apt. #

City _____ State/Prov. _____ Zip/Postal Code

Signature (if under 18, a parent or guardian must sign)

Mail to the **Reader Service:**
IN U.S.A.: P.O. Box 1867, Buffalo, NY 14240-1867
IN CANADA: P.O. Box 611, Fort Erie, Ontario L2A 9Z9

Want to try two free books from another line?
Call 1-800-873-8635 or visit www.ReaderService.com.

*Terms and prices subject to change without notice. Prices do not include applicable taxes. Sales tax applicable in N.Y. Canadian residents will be charged applicable taxes. Offer not valid in Quebec. This offer is limited to one order per household. Books received may not be as shown. Not valid for current subscribers to Harlequin Desire books. All orders subject to credit approval. Credit or debit balances in a customer's account(s) may be offset by any other outstanding balance owed by or to the customer. Please allow 4 to 6 weeks for delivery. Offer available while quantities last.

Your Privacy—The Reader Service is committed to protecting your privacy. Our Privacy Policy is available online at www.ReaderService.com or upon request from the Reader Service.

We make a portion of our mailing list available to reputable third parties that offer products we believe may interest you. If you prefer that we not exchange your name with third parties, or if you wish to clarify or modify your communication preferences, please visit us at www.ReaderService.com/consumerchoice or write to us at Reader Service Preference Service, P.O. Box 9062, Buffalo, NY 14240-9062. Include your complete name and address.

HDI7

There's no way Lola Whittaker is going to rekindle the
flames between her and sexy smoke jumper
Erik McKnight—she still hasn't forgiven him for the past.

Read on for a sneak preview of
UP IN FLAMES,
the newest Kira Sinclair title from Harlequin Blaze!

"Lola. It's good to see you."

"Erik. I can't say the same."

That wasn't strictly true. Because even as anger—
anger she'd been harboring for the last six years—burst
through her, she couldn't stop her gaze from rippling
down his body.

He was bigger—pure muscle. Considering the work he
did now, that was no surprise. Smoke jumping wasn't for
weaklings. It was, however, for daredevils and adrenaline
junkies. Erik McKnight was both.

Hurt flashed through his eyes. "I'm sorry you still feel
that way."

Wow, so he'd finally issued her an apology. Hardly for
the right reasons, though.

"What are you doing here?"

"Didn't your dad or Colt tell you?"

Her anger now had a new direction. The men in her
life were all oblivious morons.

"I'm—" his gaze pulled away, focusing on the sky
behind her "—taking a couple months off."

Six years ago she would have asked for an explanation.
Today she didn't want to care, so she kept her mouth shut.

"Came home to spend some time with Mom. Your dad's letting me pick up some shifts at the station."

Lola nodded. "Well, good luck with that." Hooking her thumb over her shoulder, she said, "I'm just gonna go…"

"Do anything that gets you far away from me."

She shrugged. He wasn't wrong, but her mother had raised her to be too polite to say so.

"You look good, Lola. I…I really am glad we ran into each other."

Was he serious? Lola stared at him for several seconds, searching his face before she realized that he was. Which made the anger bubbling up inside her finally burst free.

"Did you take a hit to the head, Erik? You act like I haven't been right here for the past six years, exactly where you left me when you ran away. Ran away when my brother was lying in a hospital bed, broken and bleeding."

"Because I put him there." Erik's gruff voice whispered over her.

"You're right. You did."

"That right there is why I left. I could see it every time you looked at me."

"See what?"

"Blame." His stark expression ripped through her. A small part of her wanted to reach out to him and offer comfort.

But he was right. She did blame him. For so many things.

Don't miss
UP IN FLAMES by Kira Sinclair,
available May 2017 wherever
Harlequin® Blaze® books and ebooks are sold.

www.Harlequin.com

EXCLUSIVE LIMITED TIME OFFER AT
www.HARLEQUIN.com

$7.99 U.S./$9.99 CAN.

$1.⁰⁰ OFF

New York Times Bestselling Author
LORI FOSTER

brings you the next sexy story in the
Body Armor series with

HARD JUSTICE

*Playing it safe has never felt so
dangerous...*

*Available March 21, 2017
Get your copy today!*

Receive $1.00 OFF the purchase price of
HARD JUSTICE by Lori Foster
when you use the coupon code below on Harlequin.com

HARDJUSTICE1

Offer valid from March 21, 2017, until April 30, 2017, on www.Harlequin.com.

Valid in the U.S.A. and Canada only. To redeem this offer, please add the print or
ebook version of HARD JUSTICE by Lori Foster to your shopping cart and then
enter the coupon code at checkout.

DISCLAIMER: Offer valid on the print or ebook version of HARD JUSTICE
by Lori Foster from March 21, 2017, at 12:01 a.m. ET until April 30, 2017,
11:59 p.m. ET at www.Harlequin.com only. The Customer will receive $1.00
OFF the list price of HARD JUSTICE by Lori Foster in print or ebook on
www.Harlequin.com with the HARDJUSTICE1 coupon code. Sales tax applied
where applicable. Quantities are limited. Valid in the U.S.A. and Canada only. All
orders subject to approval.

® and ™ are trademarks owned and used by the trademark owner and/or its licensee.

© 2017 Harlequin Enterprises Limited

www.HQNBooks.com

PHCOUPLFHB0417

Turn your love of reading into rewards you'll love with
Harlequin My Rewards

**Join for FREE today at
www.HarlequinMyRewards.com**

Earn **FREE BOOKS** of your choice.

Experience **EXCLUSIVE OFFERS** and contests.

Enjoy **BOOK RECOMMENDATIONS**
selected just for you.

PLUS! Sign up now
and get **500** points
right away!

Earn
FREE
REWARDS
HarlequinMyRewards.com
Join
Today!

MYR16R